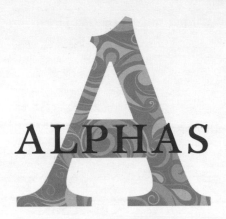

ALPHAS

Clique novels by Lisi Harrison:

THE CLIQUE

BEST FRIENDS FOR NEVER

REVENGE OF THE WANNABES

INVASION OF THE BOY SNATCHERS

THE PRETTY COMMITTEE STRIKES BACK

DIAL L FOR LOSER

IT'S NOT EASY BEING MEAN

SEALED WITH A DISS

BRATFEST AT TIFFANY'S

THE CLIQUE SUMMER COLLECTION

P.S. I LOATHE YOU

BOYS R US

Other novels by Lisi Harrison:

ALPHAS

ALPHAS

A NOVEL BY
LISI HARRISON

poppy

LITTLE, BROWN AND COMPANY
New York   Boston

"When I Grow Up," by Rodney Jerkins, James Stanley MacCarty, Smith Paul Granville
Samwell, Theron Makiel Thomas, Timothy Jamahli Thomas (Rodney Jerkins Produc-
tions, Inc., Glenwood Music Corporation/EMI Music Publishing, Inc., Universal Music
Corporation).
All rights reserved.

Poppy
Little, Brown and Company
Hachette Book Group
237 Park Avenue, New York, NY 10017

For more of your favorite series, go to www.pickapoppy.com

First Edition: August 2009

Poppy is an imprint of Little, Brown and Company
The Poppy name and logo are trademarks of Hachette Book Group, Inc.

Library of Congress Cataloging-in-Publication Data
Harrison, Lisi.
Alphas / by Lisi Harrison. —1st ed.   p. cm.
"Poppy."
Summary: Select teenaged girls are invited to join the exclusive and futuristic
Alpha Academy, where they must compete feverishly to establish and
maintain their status among their extremely competitive peers.
ISBN 978-0-316-03579-8
[1. Boarding schools—Fiction. 2. Schools—Fiction. 3. Competition
(Psychology)—Fiction. 4. Interpersonal relations—Fiction.] I. Title.
PZ7.H2527Alp 2009   [Fic]—dc22   2009019857

ISBN: 978-0-316-03579-8
10 9 8 7 6 5 4 3 2 1
CWO
Printed in the United States of America

The characters and events in this book are fictitious. Any similarity to real
persons, living or dead, is coincidental and not intended by the author.
Cover design by Andrea C. Uva and Tracy Shaw

Cover photos by Roger Moenks
Author photo by Gillian Crane

alloyentertainment
Produced by Alloy Entertainment
151 West 26th Street, New York, NY 10001

For Danielle Paige, alpha extraordinaire

ALPHA ACADEMY

Welcome to the inaugural class of Alpha Academy. Thousands of girls answered the alpha call over the last year. One hundred have been selected. The fittest shall survive.

As you know from my No. 1 best-selling autobiographies, *Watch Your Outback: An Aussie Orphan's Struggle to Endure*, *You Can't Eat Hope*, and *From Roos to Riches*, I have built a billion-dollar empire on nothing but good instincts and sheer determination—or, rather, "Shira determination," as many Fortune 500 CEOs now call it. My FEWs (Female Empowerment Workshops) have been licensed all around the world and translated into seventy languages. My cosmetics company, X-Chromosome, is the leading manufacturer in beauty products for girls, worldwide. And Brazille Enterprises . . . Well, I'll stop here.

This is about you.

While my legacy will live forever, I may not.* Should I eventually pass, I will leave behind one hundred girls forever changed by Alpha Academy. Your illustrious class is filled with hyphenates: We have an environmentalist-poetess, a dancer-model-actress, a junior Wimbledon winner–inventor, a Bollywood film star–cell phone novelist. But a true alpha is more than her résumé. She is more than perfect pitch, a perfect turnout, a perfect ten, or even a perfect IQ. She is a machine with heart. She is the future. She is you.

Survive a year at Alpha Academy and your wildest dreams will roll out before you like a giant red carpet. Orientation begins September 5. Bring your A-game and a toothbrush. Everything else will be provided. Enclosed is an aPod. It will explain the rest. Turn it on.

Sincerely,

Shira

Shira Brazille
President of Brazille Enterprises
International Alpha Female

*The status of Shira's mortality at printing time. This may change, as BE Labs gets closer to finding a cure for death.

1

There were five Skye Hamiltons in the Body Alive Dance Studio. One on each mirrored wall and one in the flesh. As in-the-flesh Skye step-turn-step-plié-step-fan-step-ball-changed, the reflections followed. So did the nine other girls in Atelier No. 1. Or at least they tried.

A trickle of sweat slithered from the base of Skye's tightly bunned blond waves down the back of her pale blue leo. She drew her shoulder blades back (even more), trying to pinch the salty snake—not because she was embarrassed, but because she could. Her body always did what it was told. All she had to do crank up the music and ask.

"And one . . . twooo . . . thu-hree . . . fourrrr . . . five . . . six . . . seh-vuuuun . . . eight." Madame Prokofiev slow-clapped to the jazzy ooze of Michael Bublé's "Fever" while scanning her students for TICS (Timing, Incongruity, Carelessness, and Smiles). As always, her scrutinizing brown eyes whizzed past Skye like two bullets aimed at someone else.

"Too wristy, Becca!" She clapped. "Less chin, Reese." Clap. "Rolllllllll the knee, Wendi. Don't poke." Clap. Clap. "And I swear on my tendons, Heidi, if you don't fix that posture, I'm going to use you as a throw pillow!"

Chignoned and clad in a no-nonsense black cami with matching flare dance pants, the aging brunette looked like a prima ballerina laced up tighter than a pair of toe shoes. Yet she moved like honey and stung like a bee.

Skye loved her.

Charged by Madame P's silent approval, Skye added a turn before the freeze, then came out of it with hands in prayer pose—a Bollywood Namaste Flower. The routine hadn't called for it—her instincts had. She'd downloaded the M.I.A. track from *Slumdog Millionaire*, and like some people got songs stuck in their heads, Skye had this one stuck in her body.

"Enough." Madame P clapped sharply, the frown lines in her passion-wrinkled forehead bunched like loose leg warmers. *Had she gone too far with her flower?*

All nine dancers stop-panted, but Skye's heart kept hitch-kicking against her rib cage. Finally, she crossed her arms over her B-minus cups and ordered it to take five.

She lined up with the rest of the DSL Daters (they made super-fast connections with boys), Missy Cambridge, Becca Brie, Leslie Lynn Rubin, and Heidi Sprout. Like Skye, her besties were blond—two in braids, two with ponies—and wore identical pink balloon skirts over gray leotards and tights (BADS Anna Pavlova Collection). Skye had added her signature sleeves—like leg warmers for arms; today's were black mesh with charms dangling from the wrists: a horseshoe for luck, a dance shoe for love, a pair of lips for kissing, and a locker key for practical reasons. Every time she moved they jingled, adding a little extra something to the otherwise humdrum musical score.

"Flair, ladies." Madame P heel-toed to the center of the room, clucking her tongue in disappointment. "Dance is not just knowing the steps. It's interpreting them." She winked at Skye, releasing her from the scold. "So please try to remember. We're doing Twyla, not *Twilight*, so stop sucking!"

Some of the girls gasped. Some giggled nervously. Skye pressed her thumb against the sharp grooves of her locker key. The pain kept her from gloat-smirking.

Madame Prokofiev snapped her fingers. "Again! And one . . . twooo . . . thu-hree . . . fourrrr . . . five . . . six . . . seh-vuuuun . . . eight."

This time, the girls responded like thoroughbreds at the starting bell. Their Capezio'd feet polished the shiny wood floor that the Hamilton family had owned for years. The force of their synchronized movements pumped Skye with energy and made her sweat pride. Not only for the girls who danced, but also for her parents, who gave them the place to do it.

A thunderous knock interrupted their flow. The door opened just enough for Madame P to see that someone wanted her in the hall. She gave Skye a nod, silently transferring power to her star pupil, and then slipped out.

Skye rolled her neck, then padded happily to the front of the class, pausing only to change songs. "Same routine in triple time." She grinned, her legs twitching, ready for some real dancing.

"When I grow up I wanna be famous I wanna be a star . . ." the Pussycat Dolls meowed from the iPod deck.

"Ah-five, six, seven, eight . . ." Skye went hard. The midday light pouring in from the windows found her like a spotlight.

Tutting, waving, popping and locking, she moved faster to the pounding beat than the Tasmanian Devil on *So You Think You Can Dance*. With Madame P gone, she could let go of the traditional dance steps and express herself freely. Borrowing at will, she riffed on a few Bollywood moves, added the punch of Broadway, a dash of Beyoncé hip-shaking, and a sprinkle of ballet scissors from *Romeo and Juliet*. She moved between more styles than a *Moulin Rouge* montage. At the end, she executed a final glissé tour jeté, leaped up, and gave a little bow to the captivated audience that would be there one day. The charms on her sleeves clanged together. They sounded like applause.

Straightening, she turned to the two rows of four behind her and panted, "Again. Without me this time."

Skye had set the barre high. Just like it had been set for her by her mother years ago. Leslie Lynn attacked the moves with gusto, but that very same headbanging enthusiasm caused her bangs to wriggle free from her loose braid. Her attempt to sideswipe them during an axel turn dropped her one second behind the other dancers and left her dragging like a piece of toilet paper on the back of a shoe.

Feet turned out in textbook first position—her power position—Skye pursed her lips and channeled her inner Russian dance dictator. "The mirrors are here for us to perfect our form, not our hair," she announced. Leslie picked up the pace with an embarrassed grimace.

"Chest out," Skye demanded of Heidi, whose posture had taken another dive. Heidi had sprouted B-plus cups this year, the pull of which she was obviously still having trouble adjusting to. "Own 'em, H!"

Heidi thrust out her boobs while her back arched in protest.

Note to self, Skye thought. *Introduce H to the new line of Martha Graham bust-minimizer tops. Give her the friends-and-family discount if she balks.*

Next to her, Becca spiked up into a high, athletic half

split that was about two centimeters short of a cheerleader hurkey. Skye pulled Becca's ponytail down to stop her over-zealous bobbing. "Less bounce, more weight."

Becca sucked in her already concave stomach on hearing the word *weight*. Skye sighed. Becca wasn't the brightest beta on the barre, but she was sweeter than Splenda and shadowed Skye with the dedication of a choral swan in *Swan Lake*. Those who can't lead follow. And as long as they followed Skye, everything was perfect.

Next, she circled Missy. Each strand of her hair was in place, just like her steps. She strung together the exquisite sequences with technical perfection: Her toe was pointed at a forty-five-degree angle, her shoulders parallel to the floor, and her leaps timed to a millisecond of the driving beat. But she was full of more lead than a Chinese toy.

The song ended and the dancers stopped. Missy blinked up at her friend, eagerly awaiting her notes. It was like a sadist's Hallmark card; when you care enough to be insulted by the very best.

"Watch me." Skye launched into a perfect piqué turn, arms wide, hands clasped, as if hugging Kevin Fat-erline. "You want to be solid and liquid at the same time, like an unopened juice box on a whirling merry-go-round," she instructed, borrowing a line from her mother and passing it off as her own.

One . . . two . . . three . . .

After the third revolution, the door creaked open and Madame P glided back in.

On the fourth turn, Skye saw her parents, dressed in matching gray-and-white *après*-dance warm-ups, her mother waving a piece of gold paper over her head.

And on the fifth—wait, was that a *camera crew*? Skye slowed, then settled on the balls of her feet. Lithe waitresses dressed in white BADS unitards and silver tutus wheeled in tray after tray of dim sum followed by Skye's favorite cake, Payard's *pont neuf*. It was a veritable port-a-party. *But why?* Food was never allowed in the studio. Or in the dancers, for that matter.

Missy and Leslie widened their glitter-dusted eyes at Skye, who shrugged in return.

"Congratulations, my darling!" Natasha Hamilton shouted in her faint Russian accent. Her moonlit whitish-blond hair was clipped in a low ponytail. But the rest of her moved with uninhibited joy. She waved a gold-glittered envelope in the air. "You have been accepted to Alpha Academy!"

The back eight squealed in envy-delight.

"*What?*" Skye's Tiffany box blue eyes searched her mom's identical ones for an explanation. A retraction. A punch line.

But the pride on her mother's face was as genuine as it was rare.

The last time Skye had seen it was seven years ago, when she'd told her mother she wanted to become a professional ballerina, just like her. Months later the studio had been built, instructors had been imported, and training had begun. But no matter how hard Skye danced for it, that proud expression had never returned. Until now.

Eccentric billionaire entertainment mogul Shira Brazille had announced the school's opening on her show, *The Brazille Hour*, last spring, and Skye had been desperate to attend ever since. The Aussie expat had founded the exclusive boarding school to nurture the next generation of exceptional dancers, writers, artists, and inventors because she was—in her and everyone else's estimation—the final word in all things alpha. CEO of AlphaGirl International, acclaimed entrepreneur, fashion guru, Shira was *everywhere*. She was more respected than Martha, more revered than Michelle, and more liked than Oprah.

Skye threw up her arms and spun in a perfect pirouette. "I'm in!" She tapped her toe on the floor, her breath catching in her throat. This was it. Her big break. The gateway to more stages, more solos, more standing ovations, more proud expressions, more chances to be at the center of everything.

A brunette reporter with a chin-butt that rivaled Demi Lovato's stood in front of a one-man camera crew. She forced a wide grin on her powder pink lips. "This is Winkie Porter from

Westchester News 1, reporting from Body Alive Dance Studio in Westchester, New York?" Winkie's voice went up at the end of every sentence, making even her name sound like a question. "Eccentric billionaire entertainment mogul Shira Brazille announced the opening of Alpha Academy last spring to, and I quote, 'nurture the next generation of exceptional talent without distractions from our mediocre world.' And our very own fourteen-year-old Skye Hamilton, dance wunderkind, is one of the lucky one hundred to secure a coveted spot!"

"You did it, Skye-High!" Her dad scooped her up into a lift, and she giggled on the way down. Even though she landed perfectly, she still felt like she was floating.

"Are we getting this?" Winkie asked her stubbly-but-cute camera guy. When he shook his head no, she said, "Mr. Hamilton, could you do that again?"

The dancers scuttled behind Skye and her father in an attempt to get on camera. They moved in a tight tangle, like a clump of hair coasting toward the shower drain.

Skye shrugged and nodded at her dad, whose hazel eyes moistened with pride as he whirled her again. He set her down gently, his full head of dark blond hair slightly tousled from the spinning. She patted it down like he was her very large obedient poodle.

"Did you ever think your daughter would be sought after by the most influential woman in the world?" Winkie stuck a microphone under his strong chin.

"Of course." Geoffrey smiled at his daughter.

Winkie rested her frosty hand on Skye's shoulder. "We heard there was a little mishap with your essay and that it was lost in the mail. Did you stay up all night rewriting? Take us through your ordeal."

Skye adjusted her sleeves. How did Winkie know about that?

She'd had received word that the essay portion of her application has been misplaced last month, but hadn't bothered to write another. She'd been too busy pursuing her other favorite pastime: boys. Skye had been hoping to discover whether surfer hawttie Dune Baxter's lips tasted like saltwater taffy, but he'd turned out to be interested in eighth grader Kristen Gregory, instead.

"It was really stressful," Skye lied. "Let's just say I have calluses on my hands to match the ones on my feet."

Winkie laughed with her mouth closed.

Behind the camera, old instructors, school friends, and neighbors were starting to arrive. Greeting one another with hugs, they stuffed dumplings in their mouths and then chew-nodded their delight in this local success story.

Winkie stuck a microphone under Skye's barely glossed lips. "Tell us how it feels to be chosen by Shira Brazille, entertainment mogul. Icon. Alpha."

Skye reached up and pulled a silver chopstick from her artful bird's nest, releasing a cascade of blond wavelets for the camera. "Shira's a real hero of mine," she said confidently. "Her outback-to-riches story is such an inspiration. It shows what a girl can do when she applies herself. And now to give back in this way—wow!" Skye inflected as if all this had just occurred to her and she hadn't practiced a million times with her mother over the summer before the essay was lost.

"And for those of us unfamiliar with the term, what exactly is an 'alpha'?" Winkie asked through her pasted-on smile, air-quoting with her microphone-free hand.

"If you have to ask, then you'll never know." Skye didn't have an edit button. Girls like her didn't need one.

Winkie's eye twitched but she moved effortlessly onto the next topic. "Skye, you are the only girl chosen from New York state. Are you nervous about no longer being a big fish in a small pond? Do you feel ready to leave this all behind?" She licked her lips, as if she'd hit her Barbara Walters cry-inducing question.

Was Skye ready? She looked around at BADS, where she was the best dancer they'd ever had, and at the DSL Daters, who had been nothing more than well-dressed Nutcrackers before she brought them to life. Skye pinched her mini lips charm between her thumb and pinkie. She'd already kissed all the Best Westies (Westchester boys). She'd always suspected she was destined for bigger things.

Natasha's bony fingers reached for her daughter's hand.

A cue to return to the script. "My mom taught me that success is like ballet. You work until your feet hurt, until your muscles ache, until your body knows the steps without thinking. You challenge yourself every day to dance harder, better, longer. So when the lights come on and the performance begins, it looks effortless. "

Her mom's round mouth and full lips moved along with her own. After a career full of interviews and TV appearances, Natasha always knew what to say. But Skye could never put her feelings into words. She was the type who had to get on her feet and show them.

"Well, you're certainly ready." Winkie's voice didn't go up that time—there was no question about it.

"Thanks for the party, Mom." Skye followed Natasha to a pair of chairs in the corner once everyone had gone. "And for rewriting my essay."

"I didn't write it." Natasha crunched down on a piece of celery. "I added a few lines here and there, but you did most of the work."

Skye studied her mother's pronounced jaw. It was pulsing from chewing, not tension. She lifted a silver box out from under her chair.

"Hmmmm." Skye looked up at the track lights. Maybe the essay had been found after all? Or maybe when the

Alpha Academy admissions committee saw her video audition, they realized she didn't need one?

Natasha handed her daughter the box and Skye slowly untied the white bow.

She lifted a lavender toe shoe from the tissue paper, its worn silver satin ribbons trailing behind like smoke from a blown-out candle. The pair had hung over her mother's vanity forever. Like stamps on a passport, the scuffs, scrapes, and frayed silk told the story of her mom's career: from *Swan Lake* at the Mariinsky Theatre in St. Petersburg, *Coppélia* at the Théâtre du Châtelet in Paris, and *Sleeping Beauty* at the Royal Opera House in London, where a grand jeté gone wrong had landed her in King's College Hospital with a torn meniscus and a fractured career.

"They're too big for me," Skye said, hoping for a new pair. Maybe something in a soft gold. "Besides . . ." She searched the box for the other shoe, but the tissue was empty. "There's only one." Skye furrowed her brow, not sure what she was supposed to do with one big used shoe.

"This slipper is special," Natasha whispered. "It will fit your hads."

"Huh?" Skye blinked. Her mom had been in the country for eighteen years, but every once in a while something got lost in translation.

"It will fit your HADs," Natasha repeated. "Your Hopes And Dreams." She flipped open the tip of the shoe. "You write what you wish for for and hide it in the shoe. When the time is right, it comes true."

"Really?" Skye leaned in closer. "What did you wish for?"

"Meeting your father," Natasha mused, untucking Skye's hair from behind her ears. Skye knew the story well. Her mom—the original DSL Dater—had come to America when she was seventeen to perform at Lincoln Center. After one dance onstage, she'd landed a marriage proposal from Skye's dad and defected. "This dance studio," Natasha continued. "And you."

Her mother's words filled her muscles with the kind of warmth that comes after a good stretch. They softened and strengthened her at the same time. Who cared how her application had landed on Shira's desk? All that mattered was that it had.

Skye glanced around at the place she'd learned to dance, suddenly feeling too big for the small studio. The leaded windows, the track lighting with special bulbs that flattered blondes, the nick in the doorjamb where she'd spun and whacked the frame with her Tinker Bell wand when she was six. They were part of her past now, destined to shrink into wallet-size snapshots in her memory. Images that she'd flip through when she needed to remember where she came from.

Weaving the shoe's silk straps through her fingers, Skye

glanced at her mom's cheekbones. Her pale skin covered them like white tights over smooth stones when she
smiled.

"You will be the best dancer at Alpha Academy." Her
mother pulled her to her heart, like their hug was choreo-
graphed. The jingle of charms made her homesick even
though she was still there. "What are you going to wish for
first?

Skye opened the secret compartment, discovering neatly
folded squares of blank, lavender-scented paper. They
smelled like home.

"I dunno," Skye lied. The truth was, she knew exactly
what she wanted. She had hoped and dreamed for it her
entire life.

HAD No. 1 was to make her mother proud.

2

At thirty-eight thousand feet above the desert, Allie Abbott tried to GPS her emotional state. It was somewhere between *wow* and *whoa, what have I done!?* Her emerald-colored contact lenses flitted around the womblike belly of the personal private plane. After two-plus hours of flying and crying, her eyes were finally dry enough to take in their surroundings.

Hammered silver coated the convex egg-shaped walls, reflecting prisms and rainbows all over the cabin.

"I'm made from sixty thousand recycled aluminum cans," the wall announced in a woman's warm British accent when she ran her fingers over its warped surface.

She Purelled immediately.

Still, Allie never would have known that she was flying "green" if the plane's automated voice didn't remind her every time she touched anything. She sank into her womblike recliner made from recycled tires. Allie liked that everything on the plane used to be something else—everything here had a fresh start, a second chance, and now, thanks to Alpha Academy, so did Allie. She took a sip of wheatgrass lemonade, Allie J's favorite.

"Barf!" she choke-shouted and then dry-heaved. The tart sludge clawed at her taste buds, and then she reflexively sucked her cheeks in.

"Problem with the wheatgrass lemonade?" asked a smooth, motherly voice over the intercom from the cockpit. It was the same voice that had welcomed her aboard. The same voice that had told her she'd be flying to a discreet location somewhere in the Mojave Desert. And the same voice that had reminded her there was no turning back as the wheels lifted off the runway in Santa Ana, California.

"Nope. The lemonade is perfect," Allie lied—a skill she'd mastered over the last few weeks. And something that she'd hopefully get even better at once she landed. Because Alpha Academy had outfitted this plane for a very different Allie Abbot. Allie J. Abbott, to be specific. The girl power poet–slash–eco-maniac songwriter. Not the heartbroken mall model who worshipped pop culture, pop songs, and Pop-Tarts. No. No one wanted that Allie these days.

Thumbing away another tear, Allie nestled into her ergonomic recliner. It was made of what looked like Bubble Wrap filled with water, and felt like getting a massage from a hundred different people at once. If her intestines weren't contracting from the shot of wheat-ass, it might have felt incredible.

"Um, hello? Can I watch a movie?" Allie asked the empty cabin. Maybe the flight attendant was sitting up front with the pilot? Suddenly the lights dimmed and an electric cart filled with organic popcorn pulled up beside her. A hemp blanket slid out of the armrest like a fax and wrapped around her entire body until she felt like a crab hand roll.

Leonardo DiCaprio's *Eleventh Hour* began immediately. "This film will be shown in high definition using patent-pending Smell-O-Vision, a feature that sprays a scent to match the image on-screen," the British voice informed her over the intercom. Just then Leo appeared on screen, accompanied by the fresh aroma of jojoba and eucalyptus, the notes in Fletcher's Intense Therapy Lip Balm.

Allie's mouth began to involuntarily pucker, longing for the taste of her ex-boyfriend's kisses. Serious-leh? If flying on a talking personal jet to the most exclusive academy in the world while committing identity theft didn't help her forget him, a lobotomy was the only remaining option.

Allie had first seen Fletcher Barton at the Riverside Palace Mall in downtown Santa Ana. They'd locked eyes on the north escalators—she was going up, he was going down. Her arms were full of bags. His were full of muscles. Goose bumps sprouted all over her spray-tanned body that had nothing to do with the frigid air-conditioning and everything to do with his leather jacket. He was tall and fit, with product-enhanced light brown hair and narrow blue eyes. She was the same. For a second, Allie wondered if they were related. Maybe fraternal twins separated at birth. But their attraction had been too strong for something that creepy.

"Wait!" he shouted, pushing past moms and their kids, taking the steps two at a time as he darted up the down escalator.

They met at the top.

"I'm Fletcher," he panted, holding out his hand.

Allie immediately put down her bags and stuffed her hands in the kangaroo pouch of her suede tunic. She pocket-pumped some Purell onto her palms and rubbed them together. Not because she thought he looked germy—in fact, he looked more sanitary than any boy she'd ever seen—but because he had been gripping the rubber rail for at least twenty seconds, and that was more than enough time for a virus to adhere to his fingertips.

"You want?" Allie extended the clear bottle.

"No, thanks." He smiled with his entire face. "I've got the wipes." He pulled a square package out of his back pocket, tore it open with his tartar-free teeth, and rubbed. With a swift toss, the used cloth soared straight into the trash can and Cupid's arrow straight into Allie's heart.

From then on they were inseparable, and quickly became known for their combined physical perfection and strong immune systems. Everyone joked that when they got married and had kids, they would be studied for advancing the human genome. Allie said it too, only she was serious.

And the best part was that her BFF, Trina, who was single, and much less attractive than them, never got jealous or made Allie choose. In fact, she seemed just as inspired by their beauty as everyone else. Always wanting to be around them and nibble on the by-product of their love. But what Trina lacked in beauty she made up for in artistic talent. She'd even offered to tag along with the couple to Disneyland for their eleven-month anniversary, and sketch picturesque moments of their enchanted day in charcoal.

"Ha!" A bitter laugh escaped Allie's waxy Burt's Bees–coated lips—the natural balm was an unfortunate favorite of Allie J's.

"Everything okay back there?" the voice asked from the cockpit.

Um, if by okay you mean wanting to shove my bare unpedicured foot up my ex-friend's butt like a shish kebab skewer, then yes, everything is fine, Allie wanted to shout. But that would blow her cover faster than a DNA sample. So she simply nodded yes and forced a smile in case the omniscient voice could see her from behind the aluminum wall.

"Good," it replied, satisfied.

But it wasn't. Nothing was good. Not since the happy

threesome had boarded the yellow-and-blue submarine on the *Finding Nemo* ride. Not since everything went dark when they had been "swallowed by a whale." Not since the lights flashed back on and Fletcher's neck was covered in charcoal fingerprints. And Trina's lips smelled like jojoba and eucalyptus. And they both looked more caught than Nemo.

Allie slammed her compact shut without the satisfying click. She just didn't get it. With puffy O-shaped lips, narrow navy blue eyes, skin that looked lit from within, and a nose so perfectly sloped that a girl two towns over had requested it for her fifteenth birthday, beauty was her backstage pass. It got her everything she ever wanted. So why hadn't it been enough to keep Fletcher? Or rather, how had she lost him to a girl who was a mere 6.5 out of 10 after Photoshop?

She'd asked him that one day after school.

"Alliecat, you're a hottie, no question." Fletch leaned back like there was a wall behind him, even though they were in the middle of the basketball court during practice. "But Trina's talent is more attractive than being a perfect ten." He caught the ball and began dribbling it down the court. Allie followed despite the angry coach and his threats to call the police. Fletcher shot and scored. His teammates smacked him high fives. In the empty stands, Trina speed-sketched the moment. Allie began to cry.

"I'm sorry." Fletcher wiped his sweaty forehead with the bottom of his jersey. "But it's not about looks for me."

"Since when?" Allie mumbled, eyeing Trina's witchy black bangs, asymmetrical brown eyes, and pressed-down nose with borderline envy. Maybe if she had been born ugly she would have had to develop a talent too. But she hadn't been. And that wasn't her fault! Yet here she was, paying the price.

"Since always," Fletcher insisted, obviously lying. Because for the last eleven months he'd had no problem posting her pictures on his Facebook page. "I want to be inspired. And she does that."

"Real-leh? How? By drawing pictures of you out of barbecue ash?" Allie felt the grip of his coach's meaty hands on her shoulder. "Her binder doodles are just another way for you to admire yourself. They're like mirrors or pictures—" The meaty hands tightened and began pushing her toward the exit. "Ow!" Allie squealed all the way to the double doors.

Once outside, she Purelled her shoulder until she heard eleven boys and one girl applauding. It sounded like a thousand tiny slaps.

Word spread quickly about the scandal, and even more quickly about their on-court battle. There was only one thing left to do.

Hide.

Allie retreated into her room with the intention of never leaving it again. She'd lost her boyfriend and best friend all in one afternoon, and the loneliness and betrayal hurt more than a lip wax. Her mom came in frequently with all her favorites from the food court. But the pit in her stomach was too deep to fill, even with Hunan Pan's crispy fried wings and pot stickers.

Until two days later, when her lo mein arrived with a heavy gold package.

Allie sat up in bed and asked her mother to kindly close the door behind her.

It's about time! She sniffled, tearing through the vellum. She wondered if Fletcher would just apologize or actually grovel, and what kind of gift he was sending to make it up to her. A gold mobile device fell onto her duvet-covered lap along with a letter. It looked like an iPod dipped in glitter. *Huh?*

Dear Allie J,
Welcome to the inaugural class of Alpha Academy . . .

Allie whipped the letter onto the ground and beat her Tinker Bell pillowcase. It figured Allie J would be hitting a high note when Allie was at her lowest.

Allie had been getting the girl's fan mail for years. The songwriter had grown up on the Applemay Farm Commune just five miles outside Santa Ana. But ever since she'd left on some save-the-melting-ice-caps mission in Antarctica, the letters had been coming more frequently. Allie could have notified the post office, but that would have involved forms and post office people. Both of which were boring and probably covered in germs. Besides, Allie J's songs had shown up on the sound tracks of three teen summer flicks, and according to a blind item in Page Six, a certain trio of Disney brothers were fighting over more than her body of work. And who knew what one of them might send. Maybe himself?

Allie lowered her head, succumbing to a new generation of tears. Through salty blurred vision the gold seal of the envelope had caught the light and winked at her from the floor. Like they shared a joke. Or a secret. Or the need to escape.

Allie raced to her laptop and Google-imaged Allie J. Only three pics came up:

1. A green eye behind a mess of black hair.

2. Her thin body photographed from behind. She was onstage, facing the audience at New York's famed Nuyorican Poets Cafe in a white dress and bare feet.

3. A grainy camera phone pic of her face with what appeared to be a very large mole.

And that was it.

It was perfect.

Allie raced to the mall for the first time in days.

Hours later, she had black hair, green contact lenses, and a kohl-mole on her left cheek. She told her parents the new look was part one of her heartbreak recovery plan. Part two was applying to Alpha Academy. They couldn't quite understand the mole, or how "catalogue modeling and a vast knowledge of mall culture" were talents Shira Brazille valued, but they went with it anyway. Sure the Academy was intended for artists, writers, and inventors, but Allie had her own gifts. She could remember the lines from any romantic comedy she'd ever seen with the accuracy of a sci-fi geek memorizing *Battlestar Galactica*. She could apply makeup like a painter. She was a veritable celebrity historian: She knew the height, weight, dating history, and clothing preference of every major star. And at least she was eating pot stickers again.

Days later, Allie waved her acceptance letter around (after gold-outing the J) and said goodbye to her supportive parents.

And here she was, a green-eyed butterfly flying toward a new beginning on a top secret mission to Get Over Him.

"Sixty seconds until we enter the communication-free zone. No texting, no phoning, no Internet," announced the British voice.

"For how long?" Allie asked the speaker above her head.

"Until you return."

"Serious-leh?"

"Fifty seconds."

What? Allie felt her stomach twirl like the food court's Jamba Juice machine. If she couldn't let Fletcher and Trina know how awesome her life was without them, what was the point? She whipped out her Samsung and began typing.

I'm on a private plane heading for Alpha Academy. This is the last time you will hear from me. Turns out I have talent after all.

Allie read it over. Did the message imply *I am fine without you? I have moved on? I have more talent than Trina?*

"Twenty seconds." A countdown appeared where Leo's face had been. It smelled like loneliness.

Allie's thumb hovered over the send button. The text was missing something, something that stung like a thousand tiny slaps. Something that—

"Nine seconds."

"Got it!" Allie half smiled, mindful of smudging her mole, and then added a few final lines.

In this world there are artists and subjects. You know, the people worth drawing? Well, I am a subject. I always will be. Capture me if you can.

—Allie

She hit SEND and dropped the obsolete phone on the lap of her secondhand white dress—apparently Emily Dickinson had worn something white every day, and so did Allie J. But even after dry-cleaning the dress nine times and liberally spraying it with Clinique Happy, Allie still smelled dead people.

"We are now in a communication-free zone," announced the voice, "and are beginning our descent to Alpha Island, where temperature on the ground is a perfect seventy-two degrees." She snickered softly. "For now."

Allie craned her neck to see the view out of the plane's mini windows to the Mojave Desert below. Joshua trees and cacti filled in the blanks between expanses of red sand. Rock formations of red clay monsters climbed on top of each other and reached for the sky, as if they, too, wanted to hitch a ride to Alpha Island. Allie triple-blinked as the desert gave way to an oasis of blue. It was as if someone had taken a giant @-shaped cookie cutter and carved out an island. Allie glimpsed white buildings beneath a canopy of palm trees, no doubt planted to provide shade from the Mojave heat and prying paparazzi.

Without warning, the plane swooped down along with Allie's stomach, as she considered what she'd gotten herself into. Sticking an earbud in each ear, she let the words from Allie J's latest hit, "Global Heartwarming," coax her into character.

Reduce, reuse, and recycle my heart
Give it back to me
'Cause I want a fresh start
Now that I'm fine,
You're on your knees
Begging me please
To be your main squeeze
You're starting to panic
Calling me satanic
But I prefer organic
And hold the cheese!
Reduce, reuse, and recycle my heart
It's ready for a brand-new start

She'd never really liked Allie J's music—she was too folksy and message-y for Allie's aerobic taste. But the lyrics to this one were spot-on. She tapped her newly short nails and continued memorizing the words, which could have been written for her—or better yet, by her. Then she touched up her mole and cranked the volume.

The jet was starting to dip. It was showtime.

3

"The temperature just went from seventy-two degrees to three thousand!" Charlie Deery loosened her metallic tie and began fanning her flushing cheeks.

"Hyperbole, Chah-lie," Bee Deery corrected her Jersey-born daughter in a proper British accent, as if exaggeration was strictly an American trait. Bee quickly reached for the sagging silver material around her daughter's neck and retied it. Not even the familiar smell of her rose-scented body cream—the only constant in Charlie's life—could soothe her today.

"Hyperbo-leave-me-alone!" Charlie swatted her mother's fussing hands and then instantly regretted it. Hurting Bee was like beating Bambi, only worse. "Sorry." She avoided her mother's kind brown eyes. "But I can't breathe."

Bee quickly scanned the area and then refastened the tie with a once-and-for-all cinch. "This is no time for a uniform violation. Not on the first day. Shira has enough stress as it is."

"What about me?" Charlie stomped her foot like a toddler, forever frustrated by her mother's efforts to please her boss at any cost, even familial asphyxiation. "I don't even go here. Who cares if I wear the stupid tie?"

"It's about respect," Bee insisted, patting her tightly wound updo. Was it held by hair spray or the power of positive thinking?

With a surrendering sigh, Bee aimed her aPod at Charlie's uniform; a platinum vest, matching tie, pleated mini in shimmering pewter, champagne-colored blouse with oversize puffed sleeves, and clear knee-high gladiator sandals with massaging soles and no–tan line technology. "Here." She pushed a button. The microscopic crystals in Charlie's shirt turned icy cool. "Better?"

"Much." Charlie smile-thanked her.

Just then, one hundred platforms unfolded from the Twizzler-shaped building behind them, with the hum of a passing golf cart. One for each Personal Alpha Plane—or PAP, as Charlie secretly joked—to park after landing.

Charlie lifted her brown eyes and searched the sun-soaked sky. Flecks of light flashed in the distance like copper-colored winks. They were getting closer.

Out on the tarmac, Shira's ground team raced onto the

tarmac wearing thick regulation jumpsuits in white patent leather. Assistants Nos. 2 through 5 were stationed up and down the runway, holding electronic clipboards that updated them on the progress of the alpha arrivals. As Shira's No. 1 assistant, Charlie's mom wore a skirt and jacket combo in the same fabric as the jumpsuits.

Suddenly Bee turned away, curling her ear toward her shoulder. "Affirmative," she reported into her Bluetooth device, which had been remodeled to look like a diamond stud earring. Charlie knew for a sad fact that she never turned it off, even when going two in the loo. She wished the loyalty stemmed from pride—Charlie had invented the fashion-forward device—but knew better. Being Shira's head assistant wasn't a job, it was lifestyle. Minus the life. And being out of reach was not an option.

"We're in position." Bee nodded, still cupping her ear. "Yes. We're on the welcome platform, above the tarmac, facing due south."

Bee's warm brown eyes zeroed in on the hem of Charlie's skirt—a prototype that would be donated to the Smithsonian as soon as the real alphas arrived and Charlie left for boarding school in Hoboken. Which was in exactly ninety minutes. The devastating reality made Charlie's stomach lurch. Or was that her heart?

"Ugh!" She wiggled, as if trying to slip out of her own skin.

"Stand still," her mom demanded, snapping an errant thread off the pleated pewter mini.

But Charlie couldn't stand still. Time was running out. In eighty-eight minutes she wouldn't just be leaving her mother, or the island she'd secretly helped design—she would be leaving *him*.

The oppressive heat suddenly blew by like a bad smell in the wind. A gray cloud mass gathered overhead, and warm droplets, the temperature of tears, began to fall. Well past caring, she didn't bother to cover the precious uniform. Instead, she slipped the aPod prototype out of her pocket and checked her messages. There were three gold heart bubbles, all from Darwin, all asking when he could see her.

For the last ten months, while Bee oversaw the construction of Alpha Island, Charlie had played *Blue Lagoon* with her fourteen-year-old boyfriend, Darwin Brazille, Shira's son. She hung out with all five Brazille brothers but had loved Darwin ever since they first napped together, twelve years ago, in the nursery on Shira's private plane. Darwin, on the other hand, claimed he'd loved her even before they met. And Charlie believed him. He'd never given her any reason not to.

Shira had met Bee at one of her first Female Empowerment Workshops, when Charlie and Darwin were both babies. Since then, they had traveled the world together, getting homeschooled by life experience and a tutor who was legally bound to make sure their education was up to conventional standards. Once Charlie turned twelve, the tutor resigned. She and Darwin successfully passed all traditional high school exams and were given the green light to sit back and enjoy the ride. A ride that, thanks to their hardworking mothers, took them to the most exotic places on the planet and left them alone to explore. A ride that filled their digital cameras with more romantic shots than a season of *The Bachelor*. A ride that, thanks to Shira, was about to end in a devastating crash.

To the rest of the world, Shira Brazille was admired and beloved. Her empire was a study in creativity, altruism, glamour, and control. She'd begun her career as a script girl on Aussie dramas and worked her way up to producer. There, she discovered that she liked creating and controlling worlds, and didn't want to just do it on screen—she wanted to do it in real life. She made the business of saving the world her ultimate production-slash-reality show. Shira was an international pop star, prom queen, and mother hen, all rolled into one. Why else would America trust her to care for and educate its most talented daughters, far away from their homes and families?

But Charlie knew better.

"She's doing it on purpose." She dabbed the corner of her eye with her champagne-colored sleeve, a flulike ache pulsing through her entire body.

"I sincerely doubt she built all this to break you and Darwin up." Bee gestured to the state-of-the-art architecture, to the palm and Joshua trees, and to the woman-made beach in front of them. Charlie narrowed her eyes at the trees as if they too were co-conspirators in the plot to ruin her life.

"Then why am I getting sent back east to some boarding school while Darwin stays here, with a pack of alpha females?"

Bee sighed, like she was tired of saying what she was about to say but would say it one last time. "Every girl at the academy has been hand-selected by Shira because of her outstanding abilities. And after giving it a lot of thought, she figured it wouldn't be fair to admit you based on family connections. Not fair to them and not fair to you."

Charlie clenched her fists, wanting to punch the fawn right out of Bambi.

"Besides, do you really think a few months apart is going to undo twelve years?" Bee raised her light arched brows and shook her head in disbelief. "Since when are you insecure about Darwin?"

"I'm not insecure about Darwin," Charlie insisted. "I'm insecure about *me*."

Charlie, despite her advanced brain and waist-length locks, always saw herself as a medium. Medium brown hair. Medium texture between a wave and a curve. Medium-size brown eyes. Medium hotness—more Aniston than Angie.

"We Deery women have a quiet beauty that sneaks up on people. At least that's what your father used to say." Bee smiled fondly at his memory.

Charlie twisted the three silver bracelets on her wrist. "Mom, guys don't want beauty that creeps. They want beauty that comes up and slaps them across the face. And that's what's about to land here. One hundred times over."

The rain stopped suddenly. Bee squinted up at the sky. The copper-colored kisses were getting bigger. "You are more talented than any of those girls, and Darwin knows that."

"Yeah, but Shira doesn't," Charlie hissed. "She has no idea that I took apart her robo-dog when I was ten and reprogrammed it to act like a cat. Or that I used to take the engines out of Darwin's electric cars and put them in my Bratz dolls so they could braid each other's hair. She doesn't know you gave my blueprints to the Alpha Academy lab and that some of this place was designed by me. Maybe if she did, she'd let me stay here with you and Darwin."

"Lower your voice," Bee whisper-snapped.

But Charlie couldn't. Her voice had been lowered for too long.

"It's not fair, Mom. This school is for inventors, too." Charlie pulled an electronic butterfly out of her wrist-pack and slowly opened her hand.

Bee couldn't help smiling at Charlie's latest creation, a

cute little iridescent creature that batted its heart-shaped wings in Charlie's palm. "What does it do?"

Charlie lowered her head, thinking of her first kiss with Darwin at the Butterfly Botanical Garden in Costa Rica. She brought her lips to its wings. All of a sudden it took flight.

"Oh, it's wonderful." Bee clapped her hands until it landed, then smiled sadly. "Your time will come, Charlie. Eventually. For now, try to remember that Shira has given us everything."

"No, she's given us everything she doesn't want."

Charlie's fingers immediately went to the three silver bracelets on her wrist. Both she and Darwin had DDs (Dead Dads) who had died in car accidents when they were babies. His had left him a roomful of vinyl records, explaining his love for music. And hers had left the bracelets, heirlooms he had inherited from his mother. Each bracelet had a cameo that opened; one held a picture of her mom, one of her dad, and one of Darwin. They were the only non-Shira-tainted thing she owned. Everything else had once been Shira's, or bought by Shira, or bought *for* Shira and never returned.

Suddenly, the sky darkened overhead and more storm clouds rolled in. Thunder crackled in the distance. The temperature dropped twenty degrees in an instant. Alpha Island was built within its own biosphere, which allowed

Shira to control every part of her environment—including the weather. Sensors in her clothing automatically altered the weather to maintain Shira's ideal body temperature. When she felt calm, skies were clear. When her body temp rose in anger, clouds and rain followed.

A clear platform, identical to the one they were standing on, rose up from the ground. Shira, hands resting on the railing like she was standing at the bow of a ship, gazed at the horizon until the platform locked into place. She turned to face Bee and Charlie; her wavy auburn hair blew as if blasted by a wind machine while her black off-the-shoulder Grecian dress remained perfectly still. As usual, round dark sunglasses concealed her eyes.

"Unbelievable!" Shira's down-under accent was outback fresh, even though she'd been off the continent for nearly two decades.

A crack of thunder startled everyone but Shira.

"What is it?" Bee cooed with dutiful concern.

"We've had a last-minute cancellation. Bee, can you believe our actress dropped out? She wouldn't have gotten that part if they hadn't heard I'd taken her on." Shira pushed her glasses up her nose. "A part in the new Clooney in Romania. No one says no to Clooney. Well, except me. And no one says no to me."

A series of perfect one-liners ran through Charlie's brain, but she remained quiet. Shira was like the human equivalent of laryngitis. Charlie wanted to bite back, but her mom's job depended on her silence.

"Bee, please let Clooney know I'm extremely disappointed." Shira sniffed. "And that he'll have to make it up to me," she added.

Bee turned away and began dialing.

Charlie's fingers started tingling. They always did when she thought up a new invention. It was her body urging her to start building. Only this time, her tongue tingled too, forcing her to speak.

"So does this mean you have an open spot?" she asked quickly, before her mother could get off the phone.

Shira slowly nodded yes.

"What are you doing?" Bee snapped her phone shut and glared at her daughter.

"She's trying to convince me to admit her. Again." Shira checked her reflection in her silver mirrored nail polish. "But we all know that's impossible."

"Why?" Charlie blurted. "Because you want me away from Darwin? Because you don't think I'm good enough—"

"Charlie!" Bee hissed.

"Well, I do question your motives for wanting to attend the academy." Shira brushed a speck of glitter off her pale forearm. "I didn't build it for girls to get their C-R-U-S-H degrees."

Charlie narrowed her brown eyes. She was about to get

exiled from Alpha Island—what did she have to lose? "I don't want to go to the academy for Darwin." *Only*, she added silently. "I want to go for me." *And him. For us!*

Shira turned to face her. "It's a moot point, lolly," she stated with feigned disappointment. "The admissions committee has strict rules about nepotism stating that anyone related to an employee cannot attend."

"But you *are* the committee!"

"That's enough, Charlotte!" Bee insisted. She turned to Shira, her scowl dissolving like Crystal Light in water. "Clooney sends his apologies. Will there be anything else, or can I release the circle-hold on the planes and prepare the ground crew for arrival? "

Shira tapped her nails against the platform railing, and the sky cleared instantly. "Unless . . ."

The single word hung in the air. Bee's eyes widened in anticipation. Charlie held her breath.

"Unless"—Shira turned toward her longtime assistant— "you resigned. Then Charlie wouldn't be related to anyone." She grinned.

"What?" Charlie locked eyes with her mother's, a barrage of sentiments passing silently between them. Bee's fluttering lids seemed to ask if this was what she really wanted. If she would be okay without her. If this would make her happy.

Charlie felt like her brain and heart were going to explode. Her mom was in a one-sided game of truth or dare with Shira, where Shira thought up outlandish dares for Bee, and Bee had signed confidentiality agreements that would prevent her from ever telling the truth or daring to call her bluff.

Until now.

"Very well." Bee stretched up to her full height of five foot two. "I quit."

"Are you kidding? Mom, you can't!" Charlie blurted. Ever since her dad died, Bee had worked birthdays, holidays, weekends—work was as much a part of Charlie's mother as afternoon tea. And as much as Charlie abhorred Shira, she wasn't sure Bee could cope without her.

"It's okay." Bee reached for her daughter's hand. Her lips were set in her *this discussion is over* line. Pride twinkled behind her brown eyes. "It's your time, Charlie. And I've been meaning to visit Mum and Dad in Manchester for twelve years. Don't you think I'm overdue?"

"Are you sure about this, Bee?" Shira asked.

Bee gave a nod.

"Very well." Shira nodded back.

It was a done deal.

A look flickered across Shira's face that Charlie had never seen before. The corners of her lips lifted. Her brows relaxed behind her glasses. Was that respect or the release of gas?

Bee pulled her daughter close and whispered into her

ear. "Everything I did was for you. You have a gift. It's time you shared it."

"But Mom, I can't—" Charlie whispered back, unable to fully process what had just happened. Within minutes, the entire course of her mother's life had changed. And for what? A boy?

"Do we have a deal?" Shira extended her arm.

Bee elbowed her daughter in the ribs. Charlie surrendered and offered her right hand.

"No." Shira shooed it away. "The other one."

"Huh?" Charlie slowly held out her left.

Shira stepped to the edge of her platform, leaned forward, and slipped a bracelet off Charlie's arm. In a single motion she popped open the cameo and removed the round picture of her son. Pleased, she handed it back.

How did you know about the photo? How did you know which bracelet it was in? How can you just take that from me? Charlie wanted to shout. But she couldn't. Her stomach was in her throat.

The sky buzzed. A fleet of gold-tinted PAPs circled overhead, waiting for clearance to land. Shira nodded at Bee. Bee signaled the crew to bring the planes in. It was her final job for Brazille Enterprises.

"As long as you're here, you will focus on your studies," Shira stated, watching her protégés descend onto the runway and roll to a stop. "Darwin is off-limits. When you break up with him, leave this conversation out of it. A true alpha makes sacrifices for her goals. And he will be your first sacrifice." She made a fist around the photo and squeezed. "Understood?"

Charlie gasped. *Break up with Darwin?* Charlie inhaled deeply, trying to steady herself with her breath. How could she lose her mom *and* Darwin, all in ten minutes? Then again, what was the alternative? Boarding school in New Jersey? A long-distance relationship with the two most important people in her life? At least now she'd be able to *see* one of them. And maybe in time, if she got the grades, Shira would see that she was good enough for her son. And her mom could get her job back and—

"Understood?" Shira pressed.

"Understood," Charlie managed.

Shira's lips curled back against her teeth. To the untrained eye, it might have looked like a smile. But Charlie knew better. It was the look of a predator preparing to devour her prey.

"Welcome to Alpha Academy."

4

Skye skipped down the plane's stairwell, downgrading her smile from high beam to low so as not to blind anyone with her excitement. Her mint, jersey-knit dance skirt ballooned up, and she shoved her hands in her skirt pockets to push it down around her long, tan legs. Just as her ballet flats made contact with the gold carpet that cut across the Jetway, the door of the private plane closed behind her.

A glass tower rose in the distance, and green caterpillar-shaped trees waved in the breeze. She arranged her white-blond wavelets behind her and blinked. Where was the welcome committee? Where was her adoring public? Where was *anyone*? She wasn't used to being alone. It was her unwritten policy to have people around her at all times. The silence made her felt a little lost and a little grown-up all at once, like the first time she'd flown by herself to visit her grandma in Florida.

45

Fishing her aPod out of her purse, she kept her eyes glued on the horizon, searching for signs of life.

"Follow the gold carpet," a honeyed Australian voice piped in.

There, on the rectangular screen of her aPod, was Shira's face framed by her famous red waves. Heel-toeing along the carpet, which sparkled like a thousand Swarovski crystals, Skye felt like Dorothy in Oz—only she never wanted to go home.

The carpet led her through a thicket of Joshua trees, and when she emerged on the other side of the green pine curtain, she found herself staring at a pink sand beach and what appeared to be miles of blue water.

"Ohmuhgud," she gasped, noticing the high-def rainbow up ahead.

WHOOOOOOO!

A translucent train that looked like a massive string of see-through pearls slithered along the sand and stopped in front of her. Skye tried to scope out the other girls, but all she saw was the back of their blowouts as they climbed inside their personal train cars.

Was a student body more alpha than OCD's even possible? And if it was, what did it look like? September *Vogue*? She was gagging to know. Or was the bitter taste of chocolate in the back of her throat the jet's mini cupcakes going AWOL after the private plane ride?

Once inside, Skye settled into an egg-shaped Lucite

chair. An identical one faced her; only it was empty. For a moment Skye tried to imagine who she would want joining her on this dreamlike adventure, if she could pick one person to fill the seat. She ran through her long list of friends, boyfriends, and dance friends. But no one from the past seemed good enough for the future. Not even her perfect mother. Not when the future looked like *this*! Why wear last year's dance shoes in next year's recital?

A small silver wheel next to the chair turned like a mini Ferris wheel, rotating an assortment of mini snacks—tiny bags of veggie chips, bite-size brownies, and those mini candy bars that kids get at Halloween—the kind Skye had never outgrown and loved year round. Miniatures made her feel like she was larger than life, like the world was in the palm of her hand.

She grabbed a tray of mini beakers filled with colored water—blue, purple, pink, and yellow—and took a sip. They looked like drinkable glow sticks and tasted like candy. Then she turned her attention to the @-shaped map that suddenly appeared before her.

A blinking gold arrow next to the words *Skye Hamilton is here* was flash-traveling from the opening of the circle toward the *a* inside. Skye fought the urge to press her glossed lips to the train's window to get a better view of the mirage-like oasis that rose out of the dusty desert. Clear water and palm trees were whisking by. She was moving!

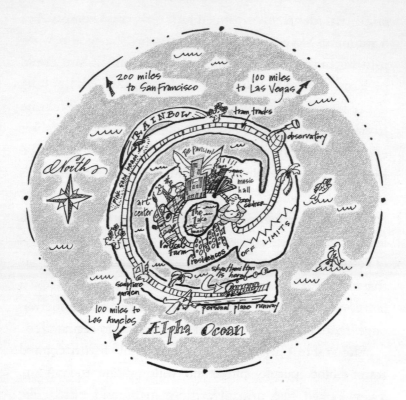

"Welcome to Alpha Academy, Skye." Shira Brazille, dressed in a single-shouldered black Grecian dress and dark round sunglasses, suddenly appeared in the other chair.

Skye gasped, and then giggled nervously.

"Oh, hi, Ms. Brazille." She choked back the bitter taste of chocolate once again. "It's a total honor to meet you!" Right hand out like a true professional, Skye leaned forward to shake Shira's hand, but her fingertips went straight through the Australian mogul and she fell to the floor.

"You cannot interface with this hologram," a stern British accent warned.

Skye straightened back up, concealing her blushing cheeks behind a wall of blond hair.

Shira cackled. "Nothing is ever what it seems, is it?" She kept laughing, like this was some practical joke they'd been pulling on each other for years.

Skye faced the window, urging her cheeks to transition from fuchsia back to rosy glow.

"My campus is inspired by the Acropolis," Shira's hologram explained as they zipped past palm leaves that turned to cherry blossoms like someone had hit "replace all." Seconds later the heavy pink blooms turned to flowering cacti.

"What is this place?" Skye marveled. She had been to the actual Acropolis and seen the ruins with her parents, but there was nothing Greek looking about the super-futuristic architecture springing up around her like pages in a pop-up book. Instead of marble structures crumbling, glass towers soared. The scenery reminded her of dancing—fluid and ever-evolving.

"Behold the Pavilion," Shira bellowed as they passed an oblong structure with white steel wings stretching out from its center, like a phoenix rising.

"It has bris soleil—sunshades that open and close depending on the amount of sunlight."

As if on cue, the building's wings began to flap, creating breezy shade.

"Ohmuhgud." Skye blinked her eyelids sharply, trying to snap a mental picture for her friends and family back home. No matter how many international dance tours her mother had been on, she had definitely never seen anything like this.

"The Pavilion is the central gathering place. Inside are the health food court, shops, lounges, the spa, and a salon. You won't need money to buy anything. Just good grades, which have a monetary value and will be immediately deposited in your personal account—you access it through your aPod. You can eat for a week off an A. But an F will leave you skinnier than salmonella. It's just like life, m'dear. You fail, you starve."

Skye giggled on the off chance that Shira was joking.

"You'll notice that all the structures here are curved." Hologram Shira pointed out the Zen Center (a giant building shaped like a cross-legged Buddha), the harp-shaped Music Hall, and the ark-shaped zoo full of endangered animals. "There are no angles at Alphas—in the architecture, anyway." Shira threw her head back and laughed. She didn't have a single filling in her entire mouth.

The train looped into the ultramodern Tokyo Times Square-esque area, located to the north of the Pavilion. WELCOME SKYE! scrolled across each electronic billboard. Then the digital letters morphed into different images of her dancing. Skye's performance at Juilliard last summer, showcases at

Body Alive, home movies of her and her mother performing a pas de deux. A cell phone video of her and the DSL Daters freestyling. Were the girls in the other bubbles seeing this, or did they have their own greatest-hits reels?

Shira's hologram gestured out the window to a vertical farm, with each floor housing a different crop, from super fruits like açaí berries to staples like green beans or those adorable little grape tomatoes. "Alphas is one hundred percent green. Solar panels power the island, and every building is smart and energy efficient."

"Just like you," Skye joked. But the hologram didn't get it. Instead, it stared straight at her with a *let me know when you're done doing amateur stand-up so I can continue* glare. "Sorry." Skye bit her bottom lip.

As the bubble train rounded another corner, rows of empty snow globe–shaped domes emerged. The train pulled closer, and Skye realized that there were no defining house numbers or street names to identify the residences, just the glittery autographs of the alpha females the houses were named for radiating off the glass.

Skye clapped her hands together. Where else would Oprah, Hillary Clinton, Beyoncé, Mother Theresa, and Virginia Woolf be neighbors?

"Welcome to your new home." Shira's image began to fade. "It may look yabbo on the outside, but trust me—it's quite different once you get in."

The doors opened with *boop*, releasing Skye and a carload of chilled air in front of a house marked JACKIE O. Waves of heat threatened to melt her like Pinkberry, but the glass door of her new home sensed her presence and slid open.

Inside, the house was divided into three floors, connected by a sweeping glass staircase that ran along the side of the circular walls. Skye raced through, squealing for joy with each new discovery. The collection of the original Jackie O's glasses encased in glass, the smart kitchen with a giant touch screen full of snack options, the home theater complete with stage and lighting board, the Vichy shower bathroom, the study lounge with massage chairs, the walk-in uniform closet filled with an array of metallic-colored separates, the lap pool!

"Hello?" Skye called, hoping to share the excitement with a real person.

Next, she headed up a seemingly floating glass staircase anchored by transparent glass to the bedroom upstairs. The space was wide open and loftlike, with a giant dome skylight that filled the room with light. Five canopied beds were arranged in a horseshoe, each dressed up in a fluffy white comforter.

"Phew," she muttered, relieved. Five beds meant five girls. She wouldn't be alone forever.

"Life is either a daring adventure or nothing," said an uplifting female voice.

"Hullo?" Heart thumping, Skye scanned the room. "Who said that?"

"Helen Keller," said the voice. "I was quoting her." An extremely tall woman in a pale yellow tunic appeared before her. Her face was surprisingly delicate, with small features framed by long, wavy blond locks. She looked like she was carved from butter.

"Um, hi?" Skye stuck her hand out in greeting, not because she was formal like that, but because she needed to know if it would go right through the woman.

It didn't.

Butter shook so firmly, Skye's fingers felt like they were being stuffed into a pointy-toe boot.

"I'm Thalia, the house muse. I will provide inspiration guidance to you and"—Thalia homed in on something behind Skye—"Allie J, our alpha poet laureate! Welcome."

Allie J, the reclusive yet beyond-successful songwriter!? Skye whiplashed around. *It was!*

She'd always assumed Allie J's reclusiveness was due to some kind of unseemly skin condition, like hairy-mole disease. But it wasn't. Her mole had total Crawford appeal, and her hair was black, shiny, and on her head. Even her bare feet seemed somewhat maintained and remarkably clean. How could someone pay so much attention to her in-person image and absolutely none to her Web presence? After all, beauty fades, but JPEGs are forever.

Skye reached for her ankle and pulled it toward her butt. A fiery sensation coursed through her quad, relaxing her instantly.

"So you're one of *those*." Allie J focused her emerald eyes on Skye. Skye released her ankle curiously. How did Allie J know Skye was a nervous stretcher?

"One of *what?*"

"A *dancer*. You can just tell. Dancers have the best posture." Allie J bent over and rubbed Purell between her toes.

"Oh." Skye giggled. "Yeah, thanks."

"Her mother is Natasha Flailenkoff," offered the muse, while sprinkling eucalyptus on the floor by their beds.

"And you're a writer?" Skye feigned ignorance. She had, of course, heard of Allie J's little book of poetry, *Greenhouse with Envy*, her chart-climbing songwriting, and her incessant eco-blogging. But she wasn't about to gush over someone who was one J away from being a single-namer.

Allie J lifted her head. Her cheeks were bright red. "Did you actually read it?" she asked, as though she had no clue *everyone* had read it.

"We kind of had to in English class. We were studying American poets and—"

"Cool, yeah, well, don't worry if you didn't finish it," Allie J interrupted. "I'm so over talking about it anyway. Just wait for the movie musical. It's pretty much the same thing, only with music."

"Don't give up," Thalia cooed, sprinkling one last handful of eucalyptus on the floor. The bedroom smelled like a Junior Mint. "To climb steep hills requires a slow pace at first. William Shakespeare."

Skye and Allie J exchanged a side-glance and giggled.

"How about some refreshments while we wait for the others?" the muse offered, heading to the stairs before they could answer.

"What's the story with the fortune cookie?" Skye whispered, claiming the bed in the center of the semicircle.

Allie J giggle-sat beside her. "Basketball player. Injured. Turned psychology major. She couldn't live her own dream, so now she's dedicated to helping other people find theirs. She's like a Lifetime movie."

"How do you know that?"

"I scanned her." Allie J wiggled her aPod. She pressed a button labeled ALPHA ID and a series of stats scrolled over the LCD display. "Point and click at anyone on campus and it gives you their profile."

"Really?" Skye fished around the inside of her bag for her new digital best friend.

"Really." Thalia called from downstairs. "You can try it out on Andrea. I hear her coming up the walk right now."

"Oh, and she has exceptional hearing," Allie J added. "It's been documented in science journals."

Before Skye could figure out how to activate her new DBF, the girl appeared at the top of the stairs, bearing a certain resemblance to an ex-supermodel–turned–talk show host, only her eyes were light brown and her monster lashes were real. "Girls, meet Andr—"

"Call me Triple Threat," the Tyra look-alike corrected.

Skye blinked, waiting for a punch line that didn't come.

"*What?*" The girl twist-wrapped her long dark hair into a ball and stabbed a gold stick through the center. Her bone structure was so sharp she could probably shave legs with her jaw. "That's what they called me at my old school and it stuck."

"What are your threats?" A petite girl with anime-big violet eyes and beehived pink hair appeared behind her, diving into the conversation with a flawless no-splash entry. She looked like Wanda from *The Fairly OddParents*.

"I'm a mo-dan-tress."

"What's that?" Allie J asked, apparently unfamiliar with the pretend-to-know-what-someone-is-talking-about-and-Google-it-later approach.

"Model-dancer-actress," explained Triple Threat, tossing her plaid straw fedora on the empty bed on the end.

Skye was about to warn her that a hat on the bed was bad luck, but *ohmuhgud*, did she really need to be *living* with another dancer? Maybe if the hat stayed, Triple would snap a limb and end up a double threat instead.

The new arrival flopped down on the bed next to Skye and covered her eyes with the back of her hand. One second later she shot up and sighed. "I've been through so much lately— leukemia, rehab, bulimia, a fire where I saved three babies and five kittens but ended up in the ER on a breathing machine . . ."

She sighed again at the memories. "But I wouldn't take back a second of it. Because it got me here. With all of you." She turned to the window slowly and started off into the distance.

Instantly, Skye felt jealous. How cool would it be to have a dark and twisted past? The press loved that sort of thing. After all, her mother had done most of her interviews *after* the accident. Without it, she'd have been just another super-talented dancer whom no one had ever heard of. Meanwhile, the worst thing that had ever happened to Skye was diving into a pool of Jell-O—a story that would make front page of the yearbook if she was lucky.

Allie J thumb-pressed the Alpha ID button and pointed it at the girl. Skye quickly did the same, reading the screen in front of her.

STAGE NAME: RENEE FORADAY. REAL NAME: RACHAEL MARTIN-MELON. GREW UP PLAYING RAYNE STORM ON THE LONG-RUNNING ABC SOAP PERFECT STORM SINCE SHE WAS BORN. AFTER BEING RECRUITED TO ATTEND ALPHA ACADEMY, SHE QUIT THE SHOW AND DYED HER HAIR PINK AS A DISPLAY OF INDEPENDENCE. HER CHARACTER IS BEING KILLED ON A DEADLY ROLLER-COASTER RIDE DURING SWEEPS WEEK; THE SCENES WILL BE SHOT WITH A BODY DOUBLE. SHE HAS LOGGED MORE ACTING DAYS THAN ANY OTHER PERSON IN THE BUSINESS AND HAS TWELVE DAYTIME EMMYS THAT SHE KEEPS IN HER PARENTS' FREEZER IN CASE OF FIRE.

"Wait!" Allie J effused. "You're Rayne Storm? I couldn't tell 'cause of the eyes and the hair, you know, since you're usually super-bronzed and brunette on the show. But I love that soap! I've never missed a single ep—"

"Really?" Skye's eyebrows shot up. "You like soaps? I thought you were all anti-TV."

"I am." The songwriter stiffened and flushed. "But, um, the producer wanted me to rewrite the opening song, so he sent me a few seasons on DVD so I could get a feel for the show."

"So you know Bethany Condon?" Renee slapped her heavily ringed hand against her heart. "She's been like a stepmother to me."

"Yeah." Allie J blushed again. "Did I say *he* sent me tapes?"

"Yip." Triple raised an over-plucked eyebrow.

"I meant *she*," Allie J insisted. "I sometimes drop my S's—you know, to conserve energy."

Skye glanced at the empty bed. Who next? The girl responsible for the Internet? A fourteen-year-old Navy SEAL? Hermione? These girls were *better* than September *Vogue*, and Skye felt like an April Fool for having thought she'd out-fabulous them just by showing up. Skye mentally wrote her next Hope And Dream.

HAD No. 2: *Survive*.

5

"Is that Nutella and bacon?" Charlie feigned disgust with video Darwin in what would soon be known as their final Skype session. She knew that a virtual breakup was loathsome, and that their relationship deserved something way more respectful. But if she could touch his almond-shaped hazel eyes, naturally highlighted hair, the tiny black freckle above his lip, or smell the cinnamon-scented toothpicks he loved to dangle from his mouth, she'd never go through with it.

"This feast was supposed to be a surprise, but consider it incentive." Darwin flashed his camera over the entire spread that Charlie knew he'd spent all morning making. Despite having a staff at his disposal, Darwin always DIYed his own gifts.

Darwin's black-and-white–striped rugby returned to full view on screen. He pushed a button on his phone, the folksy strum of an acoustic guitar flooded Charlie's eardrums and sank her heart. Funny how she suddenly loved the music she had spent a lifetime hating.

"Allie J?" Charlie asked with an eye roll.

"You know you love it," Darwin teased, trying to smile but not quite pulling it off. They had been mourning the day Charlie would return to New Jersey for months. Now he was trying to be strong for her. Soon he would need to be strong for himself, stronger than he had ever anticipated. Charlie might as well have been holding a gun behind her back, preparing to shoot him in cold blood.

She forced an equally strained happy face. "No, *you* love it. I've always preferred Lady Gaga to Mother Earth and you know it."

"Whatever." Darwin ran a hand through his sideswept bangs, something he did when he was tired of small talk. "So how soon can you get here?" He was at their favorite spot on the island. The last stretch of beach on the northeast side. Pink sand, clear water, not a hint of Shira's architecture. His blue Converse held the corners of the blanket in place should an unexpected gust suddenly blow through.

Charlie swallowed hard. "I have some awesome news and some unawesome news." She clutched her bracelets, feeling the absence of his photo through the cold silver.

"Un-awesome first," he demanded. Like her, he preferred to rip the bandage off and follow it with an ice cream chaser.

She shook her head, selfishly ignoring his request in order to savor her last seconds as Darwin Brazille's girlfriend.

"The awesome news is that your mom is letting me stay."

"No way!" Black and white stripes filled the screen as he pulled his computer into a loving embrace. "I knew the twenty-seven handwritten letters, threats to join the army, and the silent treatment would eventually get through to her."

Charlie felt like she'd swallowed a mouthful of pink sand. Her eyes welled up and her heart pumped daggers instead of blood. "Well, don't get too excited."

His smile lingered as his eyes deadened. "Whaddaya mean?"

Rip the Band-Aid. "Darwin, I . . . we . . ." Rip it! Her chest tightened like she was wearing a corset laced with guilt. "We have to end this."

"*Skype?*" Darwin tried, beginning to notice the moving men in the background, filling up boxes and removing every trace of Bee. "What's going on over there?"

Charlie took a deep breath. "My mom is leaving. Going back to Manchester. I'm staying to go to school here. I need to be on my own for a while. To focus on this incredible opportunity. Without distractions. It's not you, it's me." She delivered her lines stiffly, hoping he'd read between them and understand why she was doing this.

"You're joking, right?" Darwin punched a plate of heart-shaped muffins. "You have to be. You wouldn't just do this!"

"I would," Charlie told her shaking hands. "I have to. You know, for my education."

Darwin's features hardened. His eyes narrowed and his jaw clenched.

Charlie knew all his expressions, but she'd never seen this one. This was not the dropped-pizza-cheese-side-down frown, or the pout when they parted for the night, or the slight bottom lip poke-out that occurred when he was losing a tennis match. This one was new. It reminded her of that painting *The Scream* they'd seen at the Munch Museum in Oslo, Norway. It horrified and pained her, and she was the artist who'd made it that way.

Charlie opened her mouth, wanting to shout, *Let me explain!* But what was the point? She couldn't tell him the truth. And anything else would just deepen the wound.

"So that's it?" Darwin asked, one last glimmer of hope still flickering in his eye. "Really? You've thought about this?"

Charlie doused the glimmer by nodding yes.

"Fine. Goodbye, then. Good luck with your *incredible opportunity*."

Her screen went dark.

He was gone.

Snot bubbled from Charlie's left nostril as she burst into tears. It felt like her soul was being sucked from her body, and the lips around the straw belonged to Shira.

"Ugghhhhhh!" She wanted to storm out. Run to Darwin, press the reset button. Call her mom and have turn her jet around. Head back to Hoboken where she and Darwin would still be together—just not in person. But then there was her mom—and everything she'd given up so Charlie could be here. So she could learn at the best school in the world. So she could make something more of her life than what her mom had had. Charlie's moral compass spun around until it was pointing north again.

The moving men took this as a green light to pack up Bee's desk, the only thing still intact. Between sobs, Charlie grabbed the electronic stapler and began unscrewing the bottom. Taking things apart and putting them back together was her specialty.

She only hoped she could do the same with her and Darwin.

Charlie stood at the foot of Jackie O's glass stairs, working up the courage to climb them. The voices at the top were saying something about being destined for greatness. The voices in her head were saying, *Turn around and run!*

What had she been thinking, showing up with swollen

red eyes, stuffed sinuses, and a pocket jammed with moist tissues? This was a major first-impression moment. It was the first day of the rest of her life. The reason she'd just said goodbye to the only two people who mattered. She should be pumped. Motivated! Ready to show Shira what she was made of. And yet, Charlie couldn't bring herself to take the first step.

"Oh, hi." A tall woman in a yellow tunic—probably one of the muses her mom hired—greeted her. "I thought I heard someone breathing down here." Five metallic robes were slung over her arm. "I'm Thalia. You must be Charlie."

"Unfortunately."

The muse pouted. "Buddha says, 'You yourself, as much as anybody in the entire universe, deserve your love and affection,' and I happen to agree."

"Yeah, well, Buddha never met *me*," Charlie said flatly.

"Well, I just did, and I think you're full of marvelous potential." Thalia cupped Charlie's shoulder with surprising strength. "Let's go meet the others."

Charlie took a deep breath, urging herself to try to make the best of this. Because if she didn't, her sacrifice would be in vain, and that was something she couldn't bear.

"I found the fifth," Thalia trilled once they reached the top. "Our circle is complete. Can you feel the power?" She clenched her fists. "I can."

"Hi, I'm Charlie."

Four girls, each one more striking than the next, pointed their aPods at her, then checked their screens.

"So, Charlotte 'Charlie' Deery, you were homeschooled?" asked Pink Hair.

"Yeah."

"And you've been around the world more than three times?" asked Mole.

"Yup."

"And your mom lives in Manchester?" asked Arm Sleeves.

"Uh, yeah. Well, kind of. She's on her way."

"So what's your *thing*?" asked Supermodel.

"My thing?"

"Yeah, what got you here?" Supermodel pressed.

A controlling woman who would do anything to keep me away from her son?

Charlie shrugged. Was inventing really a "thing"? Shira used to dismiss it as a childish hobby laced with a destructive agenda. It was nothing to brag about. "I dunno, I'm pretty good with technology. What about you guys?"

"Skye, dancer."

"Renee, acclaimed actress."

"Triple Threat, model, actress, dancer."

"Cool." Charlie grinned, trying to look unjealous. "What's your name?"

"Triple Threat," the other three said together.

"Oh, sorry." Charlie felt like crying all over again.

"And I'm Allie," said Mole. "J. I mean, Allie J." She giggled.

Charlie gasped. *"The songwriter?"*

"Yup," the other three said together.

"No way." Did Shira really hate Charlie enough to recruit Darwin's favorite artist? Was that her plan? To break them up so Darwin could fall in love with Allie J? The better catch? A girl his mom approved of? Unstoppable tears began flowing from Charlie's eyes. She didn't stand a chance. Even Allie J's bare feet were beautiful.

"Oh, that's so cute, Allie," Renee cooed. "Your star power is making her cry. That always happens to me. It's so flattering."

"Are you a fan?" Allie J asked.

Charlie giggle-sniffed, then dried her eyes. "I listened to one of your songs today." *With my ex-boyfriend, Darwin. I'm sure you'll meet him soon enough,* she silently added.

The muse stepped forward and cast an apologetic glance toward Charlie. "Why don't you take that free bed on the end, beside Allie J?"

"Okay." Charlie placed a hand on her duvet, wishing she could crawl inside and cry the last bits of sadness from her eyes.

"Now that you're all here, it's time to make your uniform selections." Thalia placed a metallic robe on each bed. It was chenille soft despite its shiny surface. The red

Alpha Academy logo was sewn to the left pocket. "All alphas are required to wear the standard uniform to all academic classes." Holograms of the five girls modeling the champagne-colored blouse, silver tie, matching pleated mini, and clear gladiator sandals appeared in front of them.

"Oooooooh!"

"Wow!"

"Ah-mazing!"

"I'm gorgeous!"

Everyone but Charlie squealed with delight. This was nothing new to her.

"But for specialties like dance, drama, swim, spa, ski, gymnastics, ice skating, sports, sleep, and study, you will have these options."

The holograms came out tumbling in metallic bodysuits, skiing in gold thermals, swimming in copper bikinis, and dancing in glittery tulle tutus.

"How do we get all this stuff?" Skye speed-clapped like a windup cymbal-playing monkey.

"Point and click," singsonged Thalia. "Everything you choose goes straight to your closets."

"And where are those?" Renee asked.

"Here." Charlie hopped off her bed and pressed a recessed button on the wall. Five doors appeared, each with a different girl's name. Charlie opened hers, revealing a giant walk-in closet.

"Hey, how did you know that?" Triple Threat asked.

"Um, I—"

"She must have read the user's guide," Thalia interjected. "Something I urge you all to do as soon as possible. You will be amazed at what this campus has to offer."

"*This?*" Renee held up a Bible-thick book. "It'll take months." She flipped through the pages, then pushed it aside.

"No big." Triple shrugged. "I've had scripts twice that size."

"In bed," Allie J cracked.

Skye and Renee burst out laughing while Charlie sank deeper into the invisible sea of depression. *Did she have to be funny, too?*

"As Vince Lombardi once said, the dictionary is the only place that *success* comes before *work*."

With that, the girls returned their focus to the hologram fashion show, pointing and clicking like Annie Leibovitz. Charlie, having already seen all the options, quickly selected some pj's, sweats, and one-piece zip-up work suits, in case she ever made it back into the lab. Then she turned her attention to what really mattered.

"So, when did you apply to Alphas?" she asked Allie J.

"Um, a while ago," she answered, her eyes fixed on the bikini-clad holograms.

"What was your essay about?" Charlie looked straight ahead, so as not to appear too interested.

"You know, the environment, music, poetry," she told the buttons on her aPod.

"Do you have a boyfriend?"

Allie J slammed down her aPod and reached for her Purell. She double pumped and rubbed her hands vigorously. "What's with all the questions?"

"Sorry." Charlie rubbed her clammy forehead regretfully. "I was just making small talk."

"It's okay." Allie J softened. "I'm just trying to shop. And you know, I only like to wear white, so this is kind of hard for me."

"I hear ya." Charlie rolled her eyes, hating herself for coming on too strong. They spent the rest of the fashion show in tense silence while the other three shopped giddily.

Once it ended, Thalia returned to her place in the center of the horseshoe. "Shira's uniforms are reflective because she wants each and every one of you to remember to shine each and every day. Even in slumber."

The girls nodded as if that had been obvious.

"Too bad there aren't any boys to model our new wardrobes for." Skye smoothed her turquoise dance sleeves.

"What about the Brazille brothers?" Allie J beamed.

No!

"They go here?" Renee released her pink hair and shook it to her shoulders.

"Yup." Allie J nodded. "I saw one walking back from the beach carrying a big picnic basket. Honest-leh? He's super cute."

No! Leave him alone! Charlie wanted to scream.

"Ohmuhgud." Skye reached for her toes. "Five of them and five of us! Perfect!"

Charlie's heart beat against her chest, her ears, and her gums. She was pulsing with a dangerous mix of emotions, but she couldn't reveal that she knew the BBs. Not now.

Maybe not ever.

Charlie stood and excused herself. But when she did, something in her pocket poked sharply at her hip. She pulled it out and ran straight for the bathroom.

It was the butterfly she'd made for Darwin and its heart-shaped wings were crushed.

6

THE PAVILION
AMBROSIA BANQUET HALL
SUNDAY, SEPTEMBER 5TH
6:30 P.M.

The door to the Banquet Hall slid open. Ninety-five girls dressed in matching metallics searched for their tables inside the dome-shaped eatery. Made entirely of glass, the walls provided a 360-degree view of the constellations overhead.

"Ohmuhgud," Skye muttered. It looked more space-ship than cafeteria. She pressed her toes into the gummy soles of her clear gladiators and nervous-stretched her calves.

"This is nothing." Thalia beamed. "Follow me."

Twenty clover-shaped tables, one per house, faced a circular stage in the middle of the hall. Each time the Jackie O's passed one, a chorus of Wall*E-sounding beeps chirped through the hushed hall.

"What's happening?" Renee's violet eyes shifted frantically as girls aimed their aPods at the newcomers.

"They're checking our profiles," Charlie whispered through the side of her mouth.

Renee angled her head slightly. "My left side is much better," she mumbled to Skye.

"Not *that* profile." Allie J giggled.

Thalia stopped at the empty table between Michelle Obama house and the J. K. Rowlings. "Please take your seats," she announced from the head.

The top of the six-leaf clover was an LED screen that spelled out each girl's name, her meal, and its complete nutritional breakdown. It was clear the menu was tailored to the girls' alpha specialties and engineered to help them reach their full physical potentials. Why else would Skye be dining on protein-packed sesame-crusted seitan? Certainly not for the taste of it.

Triple peered around and sighed. "If a girl has an absolutely perfect blowout in a boy-free cafeteria, does it still make a statement?" she wondered aloud, stroking her elbow-length caramel mane.

Skye touched her carefully spiraled ringlets, not mentioning the fact that she too was feeling the early symptoms of boy withdrawal. She bit her frosted pink lip. Could lips feel lonely? Because hers did.

"A girl should want to look good for herself, not for *boys*," Allie J responded automatically. The corner of her mouth beneath her mole twitched as if the words pained her somehow.

"I couldn't have said that better myself." Thalia leaned forward and gripped Allie J's hand.

"Yes, you could have." Renee rolled her eyes. "That didn't sound convincing at all."

"Whaddaya mean?" Allie J reddened.

"The timber of your voice was low and wavering." Renee tucked a pink strand of hair behind her heavily studded ear. "You clearly didn't believe what you were saying."

"The shoulders tipped me off." Triple Threat downed her third smoothie in one gulp. "Rounded only works if you're playing homeless or anorexic."

"Look!" Allie J lifted her arm, happy to be changing the subject. An orange origami butterfly landed on her wrist and flapped its wings. "Is it paper?"

"Recycled aluminum." Charlie smiled proudly, like she'd made it herself. As if.

"Um, excuse me," squeaked a redhead with semi-translucent skin. She smelled vaguely of coq au vin. "Allie J, will you sign my paring knife?" The girl opened a wood case and pulled a three-inch blade from its blue velvet cocoon, then handed the muse a Sharpie.

All five Jackie O's scanned her immediately.

NAME: SADIE SHMOLHOLTZ. OWNER/HEAD CHEF OF UNI-CORN CHOWDER, NEW ORLEANS' HOTTEST NEW RESTAU-RANT. YOUNGEST PROFESSOR AT THE FRENCH CULINARY

INSTITUTE. AUTHOR OF NINETEEN COOKBOOKS AND SEVEN
DVDS. PERSONAL CHEF FOR DEMI AND ASHTON AT AGE
ELEVEN. HOBBIES: MODERN DANCE, JAZZ DANCE, BALLET,
TAP, SWEDISH RHYTHMICS.

Jealousy bubbled inside Skye like boiled water. Why
hadn't anyone heard of *her*?

But with a little more thought, Skye decided it was for
the best. Sadie would eventually need Allie J's songs to con-
sole her after being dumped for cooking a giant muffin top
in her pants. Not that she had one yet. The wannabe dancer
was leaner than a boiled skinless chicken breast. But with
any luck, she'd plump up soon.

The sun set abruptly and darkness filled the banquet hall
as though a dimmer switch had been lowered. The constellations brightened, casting a silver glow over the girls while
celestial music swirled around them with spellbinding profi-
ciency. Sadie instantly darted back to the Tyra table.

Shira appeared in the center of the stage in a black
column dress and sunglasses, auburn hair blowing, dress
completely still. Beneath her feet was a floating golden
hoverdisc, levitating her a full foot off the ground.

A collective gasp echoed off the glass walls.

"G'day." Shira's down-under accent lilted through the
expansive room. "Welcome to the first day of the *best* of
your lives."

The alphas applauded, ignoring frantic *quiet down* gestures from their muses.

"You are here because you are special," Shira continued, her disc floating from one side of the round stage to the other. Her black dress swirled around her ankles. "Each of you has the ability to be the top in your field and to advance the female genome for future generations. To do anything less with your gift would be a slap in the face to the Almighty She who created you. And a slap to her is a slap to me. Because I am here to finish her work and make you everything She wanted you to be."

Applause erupted. It sounded like a rainstorm.

"The Greeks gathered the best architects of their time and created something that had never existed before: a high society with a new standard of excellence. Their islands were modeled to honor the original alpha, Athena, goddess of wisdom and war," Shira declared. "*This* island is modeled to honor you, the modern-day alphas, goddesses of wisdom and *more*."

Skye's attention drifted toward a corkscrew-shaped glass staircase behind the stage. It led to a balcony with a single table overlooking the entire hall. It was a table for six, just like the others. But something set it apart. Maybe because its occupants weren't dressed in metallics. Maybe because they were talking amongst themselves instead of listening to Shira. Maybe because they were . . .

"Ohmuhgud, *guy spy!*" Skye whisper-shout-nudged Allie J.

Allie J gasped. Triple and Renee turned their heads subtly. Charlie's gaze remained fixed on Shira like a compass pointing straight to "loser."

Skye squinted and counted not one, not two, not three, but *five* gorgeous Brazille boys. Skye's heart grand jetéd, and she shared a knowing glance with her fellow alphas. Her days of feeling male-nourished were over. Guy spy with my little eye something that is hot! she typed in her aPod and sent the message to her housemates.

The Billionaire Brazille Boys, as they had been dubbed by *Us Weekly*, were international heartthrobs. Darwin was the cute, artsy one. Taz was a serial kisser, jumping from one girl's lips to the next. His twin Dingo was a notorious prankster. Melbourne was the chiseled, model-worthy hawttie. And high-IQ Sydney hid his beauty behind a pair of geek-chic glasses.

Most of the brothers wore their navy blazers with crisp white button-downs, dark jeans, and gray Converse sneakers. Taz had cut his jacket into a vest and slipped it over a wrinkled black T-shirt and ripped jeans. It was hard to tell from across the hall, but it looked like he was wearing black flip-flops. Skye rubbed a loving hand over her dance sleeves. He seemed like the kind of guy who would appreciate them.

Shira was still talking about her expectations when Skye's aPod hummed.

Renee: They're checking us out!

Triple Threat: Who cares? They look young. I like older boys.

Allie J: In bed!

Skye: Watch this.

Putting her telepathic *look at me* vibe out into the universe, Skye made extreme eye contact with Taz. A smile instantly played at the corners of his oh-so-kissable lips. She credited dance for teaching her the art of speaking without saying a word. Like preparing for a lift with a partner, Skye wanted him to know she was ready whenever he was.

Allie J: He's looking right at you!

She tossed her hair as if trying to steal the attention. But Taz's gaze remained fixed on Skye.

Skye: I have eye contact.

Renee: Well, I have a-contact.

Renee flashed her aPod. Gold conversation bubbles filled her screen. She and Taz had already exchanged hellos.

Allie J: How'dja do that?

She inched her chair closer to Renee's.

Renee: Season 9, when Rayne Storm was after Cora's killer (b4 she realized she killed Cora herself during a drinking binge) she got a job developing software so she could keep an eye on Gavin, suspect #1. Long story short, I took a six-week training course at DeVry to prepare.

Triple Threat: I did nine weeks at a Texas slaughter-house for my walk-on in *The Butcher Block.*

Skye grabbed a napkin, dipped her fork in tomato puree, and wrote:

HAD No. 3: Crush Renee and Triple like a chestnuts in a nutcracker. She hid the napkin down the back of her skirt. If her mother's ballet shoe was worth its salt, their careers would peak on *Celebrity Apprentice.*

Renee: Not sure how that helps us get the boys but thanks for sharing.

Allie J: R, write something else.

Renee wiggled her fingers, as if preparing them for the scene.

Renee: Jackie O says yo!

Allie J: In bed!

They snickered into their palms.

On the balcony the boys were huddled over Taz's aPod like it was the latest *Sports Illustrated* swimsuit issue.

Onstage, Shira cleared her throat. "And now, a word about my sons."

The boys straightened instantly. The alphas cheered and whistled like rowdy inmates. An icy breeze blew through the hall, distracting them into silence.

"Allow me to draw upon the myth of Icarus." Shira paused, allowing time for her words to circulate. "Daedalus fashioned wings out of wax and feathers to help his son Icarus escape prison. Before taking off, Daedalus warned his boy not to fly too close to the sun. Overcome by the rush of flying, Icarus soared through the sky curiously, but in the process he ignored his father's instructions and came too close to the sun, which melted the wax and loosened the feathers. Icarus kept flapping his wings but soon realized that he was only flapping his bare arms. And soon, he plunged into the sea and drowned." Shira cast her sunglassed eyes over the crowd.

"Zzzzzzzz," Skye fake-snored. "Why is she telling us about wax and feathers?"

"She's telling us the Greek myth about temptation," theater-geeked Renee.

"She's telling us not to get too confident," quipped Triple.

"She's telling us not to eat birds," Allie J tried.

"She's telling us not to date her sons," Charlie snapped.

Skye's skin prickled with doom. Or were her crush cells scrambling to find a new home?

Shira looked sternly out over the crowd. "Males are distractions and can change the course of a girl's life in an instant. So from this moment on, my boys are one hundred percent off-limits."

All the air was sucked out of the room as Skye joined ninety-eight alphas—for some reason Charlie remained mute—in a group gasp. No Brazille boys? It was like visiting Willy Wonka's Chocolate Factory and not being able to taste anything.

"My sons will take classes with you. But all other interac-

tion is forbidden. No texting, no flirting, no studying. Those
who disobey will find themselves falling much farther than
Icarus."

A few girls giggled nervously, unsure whether Shira was
joking about that last part.

"Told ya," Charlie whisper-smirked.

Renee's picked up her aPod and shook it.

Renee: It's not working. Firewalled.

Triple Threat: Crush blocked.

"But follow my rules and you will soar. Literally." Shira
grinned at the muses, who were still onstage. "Every girl who
displays exceptional alpha'tude will get flying lessons, and
eventually, the keys to her own Personal Alpha Plane."

Everyone whooped and hollered. Skye typed.

Skye: Charlie, you're good with tech, right? Break
through my firewall thingy.

She sent the text and then handed Charlie her aPod.

Charlie shook her head no.

"I want to tell them to stop contacting us," Skye
insisted.

"Oh." Charlie smiled peacefully. Her face was pretty the

way water was tasty. It got the job done but lacked pizzazz. All of her features were exactly where they should be. Her medium brown hair Pantened to her waist, and her body was slim and well proportioned. But something was missing. Probably nothing Visine and a smile couldn't fix.

After some impressive thumbnastics, Charlie returned the aPod. Skye winked her appreciation, then began texting Taz.

Skye: Icarus should have flown at night. No sun!!! C U soon.

Taz didn't text back. He didn't need to. His smile said it all.

7

The girls' aPod flashlights ricocheted through the dark like an unintentional laser show. Allie had no clue where they were going but was certain her bare feet would be torn to ribbons once they arrived. Still, running felt good. At least some part of her was moving forward.

Heavy breathing and the occasional nervous giggle were the only sounds they made until they cleared the alpha houses. Charlie had refused to join them, claiming she didn't want to break the rules on the first night. Now Allie, Skye, Renee, and Triple were sprinting through the dark night. Sleep seemed to have claimed everyone else on the island—even the light of the moon.

"Let's stop," Renee panted, finding cover under the canopy of an acacia tree.

"Not here," Allie J whisper-insisted. "We're still too close."

Skye scanned the perimeter, her turquoise eyes darting back and forth. "Why do you think Charlie didn't want to come?" Skye pulled her fingers, cracking the knuckles.

"She probably already knows that the BBBs have zero interest in her," Renee said, as she dashed from the cover of one Joshua tree to another. "Besides, she was sound asleep when we left."

"Maybe she was faking? You're not the only one who can act, you know," Triple snapped.

"Actually"—Renee rolled up the sleeves of her glistening silver nightshirt—"I am."

"Let's just keep going before someone hears us." Allie shifted from one foot to the other to keep the ground germs from sticking.

"According to this, the boys live south of here, where the circle thingy connects to the bottom of the *a*." Renee announced, studying the @-shaped map on her aPod.

"How do you know fur-sure?" Skye cracked another knuckle.

"Because it flashes 'off-limits' every time I try to get directions."

"Shhhhhhhh," Allie hissed, fearing the worst—an office-scolding from Shira. At that kind of proximity, she'd definitely realize Allie's mole was kohl. Her cover would be blown and she'd be sent to jail for identity fraud. Fletcher and Trina would become famous as the people who'd driven her to this life of deception. And they'd sell their love story to Lifetime for millions of—

"If you're so worried about getting caught, you should have stayed behind," Renee barked.

"In bed!" Triple added, mocking Allie's favorite joke.

"I need some inspiration. And danger gives me that, okay? It's part of my process," Allie managed, leaving out the part about replacing her old crush with a new one so she could have a shot at happiness. "Besides, taking a chance on romance is a dance in tight pants. It's risky but frisky. But make the right move and you're in the groove." She smiled, relieved that she remembered the lyrics to Allie J's song "Skintight" under such extreme pressure.

"I say we follow the bubble train route." Renee held her aPod to the ground, using the screen's blue glow to guide them.

A tropical breeze launched the sweet smell of gardenias, reminding Allie of the time Fletcher had sample-sprayed Hawaiian Blossom in Sephora. He'd said that one day, when they were older, they'd travel to the South Pacific and smell that scent in person. Sadly, that dream had evaporated faster than the tiny perfume drops.

"Change of plans," Skye announced. "We're going to the beach."

"Shira just got home," Renee announced even louder.

"How do you know?" Triple asked.

"You think you're the only one Taz texts?" Renee jiggled her aPod in front of Skye's full lips. "I got the message too."

Skye shot Allie a *can you believe how annoying she is?* glare. Allie replied with a *whaddaya gonna do?* shrug.

"They told Shira they're going to look for their brother Darwin." Renee thumbed the aPod screen. "Apparently he's depressed."

"Who isn't?" Allie mumbled into the darkness.

"They lit a bonfire. We have to look for the—"

"Smoke!" Triple pointed toward the northern tip of the island.

"Let's go." Renee took off, leaving the others no choice but to follow.

Shoeless, running along a dirt path in nothing but a silver nightgown and several coats of Burt's Bees balm, Allie felt more like an escaped mental patient than a seductress. She nibbled anxiously on her bottom lip. It tasted like wax, honey, and insanity.

They finally arrived at the beach. The pink sand felt cold, almost mentholated, offering much-needed relief to Allie's scraped, potentially diseased feet.

"There they are!" Skye air-applauded the distant smoldering fire.

"Let's go!" Renee slid off her silver ballet flats and charged forward.

"Wait!" Skye called, unbuckling her clear gladiators. There were dozens of clasps going up her tanned calves.

"I told you not to wear those," Renee huffed impatiently.

"Why?" Skye fussed with a strap. "Because they draw attention to my toned legs and you're jealous?"

"Stop!" Allie heard herself shout. "Why are you fighting? A boy/Is to enjoy/Not cause tension/Or dissension," she quoted the chorus of "Boy-Clott."

"She's right." Skye kicked off her sandals and dipped her manicured feet in the water. The gentle surf licked them clean. "We shouldn't let boys come between us."

"In bed!" Renee giggle-blurted.

Finally, they all cracked up. Allie had forgotten how good genuine laughter could feel.

"Listen." Triple cupped her ear.

Their laughter ceased.

"Burn. It! Burn. It! Burn. It!"

"Come on!" Skye shouted.

The girls hurried toward the male voices, trepidation and excitement fueling their pounding hearts.

Stopping short of the flickering orange light, Allie, Renee, Triple, and Skye examined the brothers' shadowy profiles. Sixteen-year-old Melbourne, fifteen-year-old Sydney, fourteen-year-old Darwin and thirteen-year-old twins Taz and Dingo, each in a Crayola-colored hoodie, stood around a flickering fire.

"Burn. It! Burn. It! Burn. It!" they shouted at Darwin. He was hug-rocking a white sweatshirt like it was a new-born teddy bear.

Allie twisted her jet-black glossy hair over one shoulder. Were they interrupting some bizarre boy-cult ritual?

"Come on, Dar, you can do it," Taz said gruffly but gently. But Darwin just shook his head and tried to walk away. The other brothers turned to grab him, and realized immediately that they had an audience.

"Hey boys," Skye trilled.

The BBBs made the split-second transformation from boys to men. They straightened up and walked over, each one offering a variation on the standard-issue *what's up?* head nod. While her friends hair-tossed and smiled, Allie felt a sudden wave of lightheadedness that had nothing to do with her meat-free stomach. If only Fletcher could see her now. . . .

Taz stepped forward wearing a smile that deepened into a dimple on his right cheek. "We were just helping out our bro."

Melbourne pushed down his hoodie. "His girlfriend dumped him. Skype-and-run. Brutal."

Sydney made a sniffling sound. Was he crying about his brother's breakup?

Renee pinched her cheeks for a burst of color. "Who do you want, Allie J?" she whispered.

Fletcher, she answered in her head.

"Did you know your pj's are like a mirror?" Melbourne told his reflection, which just so happened to be over Allie's boobs. "I can totally see myself."

"Ignore him. He's in love with himself." Dingo extended his right arm.

"Allie." She reached for it and shook. "J."

"Ouch." He winced. "Strong grip."

"Really?" Allie dove into his grass green eyes and rolled around like a happy puppy. Until she heard a crack.

"Ahhhhhhh!" Dingo shouted.

"Ahhhh!" Allie shouted back as his arm fell out of his sleeve and landed with a thud in the sand. Blood sprayed like Evian mist. "Ahhhhhhhhhhhhhhhh!"

Everyone burst out laughing. Except Allie, who wiped his fake-hand germs on the side of her nightgown, cursing herself for forgetting the Purell.

"I've always wanted to learn how to do that." Triple tapped on Melbourne's sleeve.

"What?" he asked.

"Look *that* good in a hoodie." She smiled.

"I bet you do." He unzipped his hoodie and handed it to her. "Try it."

"Smells gooooood," Triple purred, slipping it on.

Allie rolled her fake green eyes and shuffled toward the warmth of the fire. Skye had already partnered off with

Taz, and Renee was discussing her character's emotional arc with Sydney. The last thing her heartache needed to witness was budding romance. It was more nauseating than ipecac. Heavy with hopelessness, Allie sat across from Darwin. With his drooping brows, slumped shoulders, and deep heaving sighs, his outsides matched her insides.

Totally unfazed by her arrival, he pressed his white earbuds deeper into his ears and picked up the guitar leaning next to him.

What?

More than anything, Allie was embarrassed by his lack of interest. What if the other girls saw them sitting like a couple of monks? What if word spread to the mainland that Allie couldn't score? What if Fletcher heard about it? He'd never want her back.

But Allie had never made the first move. She never had to. Allie J, on the other hand, was a different story. Allie J wasn't as pretty as Allie. She wasn't even *blond*!

Without further hesitation, Allie pulled the earbuds out of his ears and smiled.

"Did you know that however long you date someone, it takes half that long to get over them?"

Darwin popped a toothpick in his mouth. It smelled like cinnamon. "Then I'll be fine in about six years, ten days, twelve hours, thirty-eight minutes."

Hazel eyes. Sideswept bangs. A black freckle above his lip. Presumably real.

"Where'd you hear that, anyway?" Darwin asked with a skeptical chuckle.

"Um, my parents are scientists. For the mind and stuff." Allie shrugged. Actually she'd read the heartbreak-to-time ratio in *Seventeen* magazine, but he didn't need to know that.

She inched closer, placing herself within accidental knee-grazing distance.

He turned to face her, and she inhaled the citrus-y scent of Burberry cologne. It made her eyes water. Fletcher wore cologne.

"I'm Darwin." He grinned at her mole.

Allie instantly covered it with her hand.

"Allie. I mean, Allie J."

His hazel eyes looked lit from within. "The singer-song-writer-poet?"

She nodded.

"I was literally just listening to you. 'Three-second rule for your heart/Pick it up fast/Watch it restart.'" He held up an earbud as proof. "See?"

The folksy track sounded tinny through the head-phones.

She changed the topic by pointing to the small white sweatshirt in his lap. "Did it shrink?"

"No, it's my ex's." His lips curved into a painful frown. "My brothers wanted me to toss it in the bonfire. But I can't."

"Ah," Allie sympathized. "I just went through a breakup too." She pulled a dark lock of hair and inspected it. "And I got rid of everything." *Including me.*

"That singer guy?"

Allie sighed. Stupid *Us Weekly.* "No. That was a rumor. My ex cheated on me. One day I found him all over Trin—" *Oops!* Allie inhaled quickly. "Uh, I mean, all over a triple-meat burrito."

Darwin burst out laughing. It was a nice laugh—low and rumbly, but genuine. "You dumped your boyfriend because he cheated on you with a *burrito?*"

Allie blushed right down to her kohl-mole. "Well, he lied to me about, um, being a vegan. It's a betrayal of trust, really. If he's eating meat, what else is he not telling me?"

Darwin nodded like he got the betrayal part.

Allie boldly snatched the sweatshirt out of Darwin's hands. "Who cares about the hows or whys. We already said our goodbyes." She dangled it in front of the fire.

"'Love on a Compost Heap'! Great song." He gazed into her colored contacts. She wanted to look away to protect her identity. But she couldn't seem to do it. He was a magnet. She was a fridge.

"You know what, you're right." With a catlike swipe, he

snatched the sweatshirt out of Allie's hands and whipped it into the fire.

They stared as the synthetic fibers hissed and melted into a thing of the past.

"Yeahhhhhhhhhhh!" the brothers cheered on his behalf.

Darwin saluted them with a smirk, then turned back to face Allie.

Flames reflected in his eyes, but he still looked kind.

All of a sudden, the aPods began to beep in surround sound.

"What's going on?" Allie asked.

"She knows something," Darwin mumbled.

Allie's stomach lurched. "Wha'do we do?"

Darwin and his brothers raced around the beach, dousing the fire and washing any traces of perfume from their bodies.

"Turn your aPods off! Maybe we can stop her from triangulating!" Darwin shouted.

Allie J had no idea what *triangulating* meant, but it updated his status from rebound to crush.

"We have to go," Renee barked. "Now. Move!"

Skye gave Taz a peck on his cheek. Melbourne reached to pull Triple closer, but she took off before he could plant one on her lips.

Allie jumped to her bare feet.

"Wait." Darwin stepped into his gray Converse. "Maybe you could—"

"Yes!" She blushed, suddenly missing the dark.

"—help me write a song?" It was his turn to blush.

"Anytime!" Allie jogged backward, trying to commit his perfect face to memory.

"Allie J!" Renee called, running.

"Coming!" She smile-waved goodbye, then turned and bolted.

Allie had no idea how to write a song. No idea if she was about to get busted. No idea if she'd ever see Darwin again. All she did know was that Fletcher hadn't popped into her head for an entire minute, making this illegal outing totally worth it, no matter *what* happened next.

8

Charlie lay flat on her back, cursing the morning rays that cast cheerful yellow streaks across her bedding. She squeezed her eyelids shut in a futile attempt to keep the light out and the sleep in. But it wasn't the sun's fault she'd barely slept a wink. Instead of counting sheep, she'd spent half the night counting the ways she missed Darwin:

One: the smell of cinnamon. Two: his passion for everything. Three: the way he understood her, even when she didn't understand herself. Four: their endless catalogue of inside jokes. Five: his loyalty. Six: their ongoing fight over who had better taste in music. Seven: OMG: Music! He loved Allie J! Eight: She snuck out to see him! Nine: What if she made it? Ten: What if they hung out? Eleven: What if he started falling for more than her lyrics?

These thoughts kept her up all night, especially seven through eleven. How could she have overlooked the fact

95

that Darwin's favorite *female* artist was about to make a special appearance in his *house*!?

When her roommates came home, Charlie pretended to be asleep, all the while straining to hear any mention of Darwin. Aside from a few terse whispers and occasional giggles, the girls fell silently into bed. Charlie reassured her racing heart and sinking stomach that Dar had probably spent the whole time sulking, playing guitar, and wondering where it all went wrong. But that was the Darwin she knew. Who had he become in their hours apart?

Suddenly, Charlie's aPod vibrated. Her lids fluttered open.

He missed her too!

She swiped the phone eagerly from her bedside table and blinked to focus. Blinking back was a message from Shira.

SHIRA: MY OFFICE. NOW. DON'T WAKE THE OTHERS.

Even the font looked angry.

What could she possibly want? Charlie was fresh out of moms and boyfriends to sacrifice.

Drawing on every ounce of courage she had, Charlie swung herself out of bed, legs first. But instead of landing in plush silver slippers, she touched down on something mushy and tepid. *Sea foam? Animal poo? Her love life?*

Peering over her knees in fear and trepidation, she checked the floor. *Charlie Brown-nose* was spelled out in disintegrating shaving cream alongside her bed. Her heart lurched. Her eyes stung. Her stomach locked. She quickly surveyed the room, wondering if Triple had been tagged too.

She hadn't.

Four sets of limp arms and legs were strewn across the beds, as if waiting to be stuffed at the build-an-alpha workshop.

Tears burned Charlie's tired eyes like expired mascara. Why was she doing this again? With no friends, no family, and no boyfriend, the reason was starting to escape her. All summer, she had fantasized about going to Alpha Academy, surrounded by intelligent girls who worked hard and just wanted to be their best—like her. She would finally fit in with someone other than Darwin. Finally be known as something other than Shira's assistant's daughter. It had never occurred to her that she'd stay an outsider on the inside too.

Charlie wiped her feet on the rug next to Renee's bed. Given that Rayne had once had a shaving cream fight with her ex, Lance Firerock, on *Perfect Storm*, Charlie's alpha dollars were on her.

Her aPod vibrated again.

SHIRA: WHY AREN'T YOU HERE?

Slipping a short platinum robe over her silver baby-dolls, Charlie ran out into the morning. The sun was high, as if up for hours. Still, eggplant-colored clouds gathered with force above Shira's mansion.

The instant her slippered feet touched the smooth brick path, a bubble train pulled up alongside her. Zipping along the pink-sand coast, Charlie tried to convince herself that the Jackie O's weren't worth her time or energy. That she wasn't there to find BFFs, but after a lifetime of globe-trotting and homeschooling, "friends" were something she ached to try.

The chairlift stopped suddenly in the waiting room outside Shira's office.

"Morning, Charlie." Fiona, Shira's former No. 2—who Charlie guessed was now No. 1—greeted her. Her mud brown eyes and scraggly strawberry blond waves made her look like a Cavalier King Charles spaniel. She was wearing the same Bluetooth headset and hyper-alert expression that Charlie's mother had worn for the last twelve years.

"Hi Fiona." Charlie slid off the chairlift and into the familiar scent of espresso, gardenias, and guava-enhanced glass cleaner. It used to smell like home. Now it just reminded her of what she had—or rather, what was gone.

Alpha Academy news scrolled across the floor-to-ceiling windows like the ticker on CNN. *Samantha Hays, Havilland Marie, and Cindy Shure caught in chemistry lab making makeup. Formulas were flawless but the edible blush has been confiscated . . . Discovery Channel reporter from Oprah House caught trying to wrestle a lion after someone said she was no Bindi Irwin . . . The silver cami and matching boy shorts outsold the other pajama options by 30 percent. . . .*

Charlie stared, waiting for news about Allie J and Darwin, but thankfully, nothing appeared.

Yet.

"Italian roast?" Fiona placed a white mug in front of Charlie. A brown stream peed down from the ceiling, filling it to the brim.

"Thanks." Charlie sipped reluctantly, keeping one eye trained on the ticker. The bitter liquid washed over her tongue. It was nothing like her mom's, which awakened each taste bud and brain cell with a warm, spicy hello. Charlie took another sip. Little did Shira know that her specially-flown-in-from-Guatemala green coffee beans were never used by Bee Deery. Instead, instant coffee with a hint of cayenne pepper and maple syrup comprised Shira's hourly fix.

"What do you think? Is it even close to Bee's? I've tried everything, but Shira's not happy." Fiona adjusted her Bluetooth. "I'm thinking of sending the cappuccino maker off for analysis."

"Is that why I'm here?" Charlie set her cup down. At least Shira was suffering in some small way. "The coffee?"

"Not exactly." Fiona quickly pressed a button on her aPod. Platinum drapes rose up from the floor and blocked the academy's news feed, and thus any hints as to why Charlie had been summoned. Compensating for the sudden darkness, the floor illuminated, casting a hellish glow across the futuristic décor.

Fiona touched her headset and nodded. "Yes, Shira." She turned to Charlie. "You can go in now."

A panel in the wall slid up. Shira's fine red hair was up in a high ponytail, and her skinny-but-muscled body was covered in a navy terry warm-up suit. Charlie wondered if there was a spin class in her native hell. Standing across from Shira, Charlie could see herself reflected in the mogul's dark lenses. Shoulders hanging heavily at her sides, she already looked defeated.

From behind her Lucite Australia-shaped desk, Shira was spinning her black-on-white globe. Lit with red dots, it showed the places Brazille Enterprises had set up companies or headquarters. As a little girl, Charlie had thought of Shira as a fairy godmother. She'd watch with wonder when Shira spun the globe, her eyes closed, dropping a manicured nail on the orb. *Poof!* They'd be transported to wherever her finger had landed. Charlie scoffed at the memory.

Finger poised midair, Shira touched down on Italy.

"Oh, you kids did love Florence." She twirled her red ponytail. "Not many twelve-year-olds appreciate it."

Charlie clenched her teeth, barring her mouth from speaking her mind. She knew this small talk was a tactic to make Charlie sweat. Sweat into a squishy malleable lump so she could be molded into utter compliance. But compliance with what?

"The other boys snuck their skateboards into the Uffizi, but you and Darwin stood in front of Botticelli's *Birth of Venus* for hours." Shira swiped her full cup of coffee aside. "He just loved that painting!"

Correction! Dar loved me—not the painting!

"Did you try the Italian roast? It's terrible."

"I prefer my mom's," Charlie stated flatly, ready to get whatever this was over with. "I'm staying away from Darwin if that's what you're worried about."

Shira forced down another sip and then winced in disdain. "Too meek." She put down the cup. Charlie was pretty sure that wasn't all she was putting down.

Girly giggles suddenly filled the office. Shira peered over Charlie's shoulder, shaking her head disapprovingly. Charlie swiveled to face a video of her suite mates, aPods in hand, racing across the beach. A wave of relief crashed inside Charlie's chest. Maybe they hadn't gone to Darwin's after all!

"What does violating the civil rights of my roommates have to do with me?"

"There are some things that surveillance cameras simply

101

can't capture. I'm guessing Renee disabled the Alpha Positioning System. She is so Method. But I need to know who the ringleader was of this little field trip."

Charlie's ears began to ring. So *that* was why she was here. Just when she'd thought there was nothing more Shira could do to degrade her, she'd found one last way. It was like a vampire asking for a napkin after bleeding her dry.

"You want me to tattle?"

Shira reclined into in her black shock chair. It hissed and then acquiesced. "*Tattle* is such a childish word. I'm asking you to educate me"—she grin-paused—"the way I've offered to educate you."

"*Offered?*" Charlie shook her head in disbelief, the picture becoming HD clear. If Darwin and Bee were the price of admission, this was the first tuition bill.

"Come on, Charlie Brown-nose. These girls aren't your friends. You know that."

Charlie's cheeks burned with shame. "If you know all this, why do you need me?"

"There are blind spots," Shira explained, shutting off the video. "And I need someone I can trust."

"You promised to treat me like the other girls."

"I promised to let you into Alpha Academy. Nothing more." Shira gave her a *too bad you didn't read the fine print* leer.

Shira was trusted by billions. She ran Female Empowerment Workshops, funded girls' scholarships, backed women-owned start-ups. But for all her success and generosity, Shira didn't have any real girlfriends. She'd always said that friendship was the only luxury she couldn't afford. But just because something was beyond Shira's price point didn't mean it had to be out of Charlie's. And just like that, she felt the tide of anger ebb and her sense of power flow. Shira *needed* her.

"I won't do it. A true alpha doesn't step on others when climbing to the top. She doesn't have to." Charlie chin-pointed to on the copy of *Audacity: The Shira Brazille Story* on the floating shelf behind her desk. "Page five hundred twenty-seven."

Shira blinked. Once, twice, three times. Then a soothing British-accented voice sounded throughout the campus. "First period commences in thirty minutes." Charlie fought back a wave of homesickness. The voice was her mother's.

Shira cleared her throat. "Better go put on your uniform." She lifted a gold stick off her desk and began twirling it over her thumb like a mini baton. The skeleton key unlocked every door on campus, including the underground passages, which provided a stealth way for Shira to traverse the campus. If only Charlie knew a way to lock her in there for good.

Charlie stood, slightly dizzy. "Sorry. I wish I could help," she tried, not wanting to burn the only bridge that connected her to Darwin. She backed toward the exit.

"But you *can.*" Shira slammed the key on her desk, somewhere between Brisbane and Barossa Valley. "You have until noon today to give me a name."

"What if I can't?" Charlie asked, her palms pressed against the doorframe.

"There's no *can't* in 'alpha.' Just *a-ha!*" Shira smirked. "Page forty-nine." She pressed a button near the Great Barrier Reef and the door began to lower. "G'day."

Charlie managed to slip out just before it sliced her head off. Too bad she couldn't say the same for Shira.

9

Allie faced one of the five pendant mirrors in the Jackie O bathroom. Being the fairest of them all used to be the only thing she wanted. But staying up all night trying to write a song for Darwin had made her want to trade a little of that beauty for the talent Allie J had. She hadn't even been able to make it through the chorus before running out of words that rhymed with *Brazille*.

Leaning in, she inspected her roots. She'd washed a little Allie J away in the shower this morning, but her part was still intact. Beneath the mirror, the glass sink was filled with fakeover beauty products and concealed with a towel.

"First period commences in thirty minutes," announced a British woman's voice.

A chorus of sleepy moans came from the bedroom.

"The future starts when we wake up in the morning," Thalia chirped. "Does anyone know who said that?"

"You?" mumbled Skye, her eyes probably still closed.

The other girls giggled lazily.

"Miles Davis," Thalia announced with vim.

Allie hurried through the rest of her fakeover regimen before the other girls stormed in.

Mole? Check. Green contacts? Check. Blond roots covered? Check. Bare feet? Unfortunately, check.

The girls rushed in, wrapped in matching bathrobes and displaying various stages of hair trauma. Skye's blond curls were now bed-dreads, and Renee's pink updo was a down-don't. Triple's long straight extensions were still perfectly intact, just like the rest of her.

"Where's Charlie?" Allie asked, suddenly terrified she was hiding in one of the stalls, watching her transformation. She *had* seemed suspicious.

"No clue." Skye splashed water on her face. "She was gone when we woke up."

"Perhaps she had an unfortunate accident with some shaving cream." Renee lifted an eyebrow and tapped her chin, playing the villainess.

Skye giggled. Allie J wanted to. But she was too paranoid. Had Charlie heard her showering at six fifteen? Smelled the toxic traces of black hair dye? Noticed that her left contact had gone AWOL on the floor for at least six minutes?

One by one, Triple kicked open the five stalls, toes

pointed, legs straight. "Nope. Not in there. Maybe she's turning us in?"

Skye, Renee, and Allie exchanged a terrified glance. But so far there had been no word of the beach-breach. And if everything stayed that way, they could go for round two tonight.

"Hey Triple, how long have you had back problems?" Skye asked with a mouth full of toothpaste.

"I don't have back problems." Triple sauntered to her sink.

"Oh." Skye spit. "I thought, you know, 'cause your line is a little off. Sorry." She spit again. "My bad."

Suddenly, Shira's face appeared in their mirrors. Her auburn hair was in a sleek ponytail, her black glasses firmly in position.

"Ahhhhhhh!" they all screamed.

"G'day," she snickered. "No need to panic."

Allie waved her hand in front of the glass, wondering if Shira could actually see them. But Shira didn't wave back. Instead, she cleared her throat and continued.

"William Shakespeare once said, 'We know what we are, but know not what we may be.' Well, what you may be starts today."

"Is she looking at us?" Skye asked, finger-combing her hair.

"Doubt it," Allie scoffed, pretending she hadn't just wondered the same thing.

"Your schedules, like your meals, have been tailored to maximize your potential. At Alphas, I expect you to hone your talents, but also to stretch in ways you'd never imagined."

"No problem there," Triple grunted, lifting her leg over her head.

Skye rolled her turquoise eyes.

"There will be no transfers, no add/drops, and no exceptions. Good luck and g'day." Shira was gone and the mirrors returned to their regularly scheduled makeup sessions.

The girls' aPods beeped, and they raced to retrieve them from the bedroom. Allie lifted hers from the sink once everyone had gone.

On-screen, a bronze envelope with an A seal opened, and a virtual schedule slid out. Every hour of her school day was mapped out in a grid.

Time	Class	Location
7:30 a.m.	BREAKFAST AND MOTIVATIONAL LECTURE Every day you will receive a lecture from a different muse. The series is designed to inspire, motivate, and prepare your spirit for life's daily challenges—of which there will be many.	Pavilion
8:40 a.m.	ROMANCE LANGUAGES Learn to speak, read, write, and rhyme in the most romantic languages of our time.	Sculpture Garden

9:40 am	**PROTEIN BREAK** Nourish your mind and body with a personalized protein snack and feel the rush.	Health Food Court
10:10 a.m.	**THE ART OF EXCELLENCE** Learn social protocols, style tips, and conversation topics that will distinguish you from the mainlanders.	Elizabeth I Lecture Hall
12:00 p.m.	**LUNCH AND SYMPHONY** Our string and brass majors will serenade you with world-renowned compositions. Muses will whisper subliminal messages throughout.	Pavilion
1:10 p.m.	**HONE IT: FOR WRITERS** Master your craft.	The Fuselage
2:30 p.m.	**GREENER PASTURES** Save the earth without being a stick-in-the-mud.	Biosphere
3:40 p.m.	**SPOTLIGHT TRAINING** Learn how to answer interview questions and pose for the paparazzi.	Delphi Observatory
5:00 p.m.	**SWEAT** Personal training session designed to push your physical boundaries. Daily weigh-ins and muscle checks required. Dress to progress.	Buddha Building

Serious-leh? All that in one day? Wasn't studying Allie J a full course load in itself?

The Jackie O's rushed back in, uniformed and comparing

schedules. They flatironed, eyelined, and spritzed in record time.

"Allie J, come on!" Skye zipped up her makeup bag. "You're not even dressed."

Allie placed a protective hand on her towel-covered stash. "Go without me. I'll catch up."

Once the girls were gone, Allie quickly hid her things, got dressed, and checked herself in the mirror one last time. A girl with green eyes, black hair, silver uniform, and a cheek mole stared back at her. Allie covered her mouth and tittered. *Was she really doing this?*

This inside joke was far more delicious than anything she ever shared with Trina . . .

. . . except Fletcher.

A fresh wave of heartbreak sucker punched Allie right in the gut. She hated that they could hurt her from hundreds of miles away. If only he could see how good her legs looked in the pleated mini. Or what a crazy stunt she was pulling. Or how bad Trina's skin got when she was PMS-ing. OMG! What if he did know and he was over her? What if he broke up with her already? What if he was trying to contact . . .

Magically, as if summoned from beyond, the lyrics to "Three-Second Rule" popped into her head, imploring her to move on.

Three-second rule for the heart

You lifted me up, out of the dark.
I have a second chance at a life that's new,
A life that, maybe, might include you.

Was Allie J actually living inside her? Or was the song really playing?

Confused, she kicked off her slippers and followed the music outside and around to the side of the villa, where a patch of green grass was surrounded by rosebushes. Her movements were slow and cautious, like a babysitter in a horror movie investigating a mysterious noise.

Allie gasped, covering her mouth in surprise. There, under the pink cherry blossoms, was—

"Darwin!" she blurted.

"Hey." He lifted his eyes but kept playing the guitar. The plant life swayed as if holding out invisible cell phones to the beat.

"What are you doing here?" she asked, unable to conceal her beaming smile.

He was dressed in uniform, shirt half tucked in, sun-kissed hair sideswept, surrounded by a breakfast picnic. Allie studied his hazel stunners for residual signs of love-sickness. But there was nothing mopey about his flirty smile. Allie's eyes felt hot behind her green contact lenses. No one had ever done anything like this for her. Fletcher's idea of romance was a *hey shorty* text message or a fro-yo shake because they were both on the Sugar Busters diet.

"You said you'd help me write a song, oh brilliant one." He held out his guitar and lowered his head in reverence.

Allie giggled nervously.

"I can't teach you *now*," she managed, willing him to lower the complicated instrument. "I'm supposed to go to breakfast."

"Why?" Darwin lifted a croissant. "Everything you could possibly want is right here."

He had a point.

"Where did you get this stuff?" Allie marveled at the stack of pancakes, the assortment of cheeses, fruits, syrups, and what looked like some kind of vegan wheat-meat.

"I made it." He beamed.

"Really?" Allie squinted as if trying to discern a mirage. *What kind of idiot dumped Darwin Brazille?*

"Yeah." He popped a giant red grape in his mouth and chewed. His mole rode his lip like a jockey. "Why is that so hard to believe?"

"I dunno." *Um, because the only thing Fletcher ever made me was depressed!*

"Come sit." He put the guitar aside and patted the red blanket.

Allie looked around for snitches, but the street was empty. "'Kay, why not?"

"So." He handed her a plate. "Did you get into any trouble last night?"

Allie shook her head no, wondering what he would think of her natural blond hair. "You?"

"Nothing." He shrugged. "It was probably another one of Dingo's stupid jokes."

"I guess that means we can do it again." Allie took a pancake, ripped off a piece, and stuck it in her mouth. She didn't figure Miss Barefoot to be one for manners.

"How come the other girl in your villa didn't come?" Appearing lost in thought, he pressed a finger in the tread of his Converse.

Serious-leh? Did he have any idea how many germs were on there?

"Charlie Brown-nose didn't want to break the rules." Allie paused, a wave of prickly heat passed through her body. "Why? We weren't good enough for you?"

"No!" He snapped back to reality. "That's not what I'm saying at all. I was, you know, just hoping that she doesn't tell on you."

"Breakfast will commence in five minutes, followed by the first class of the day," announced the British woman.

The voice seemed to draw him back to that distant place, but only for a second.

A heart-flutter urged Allie to make a run for it. But truth be told, she hadn't signed up for Alpha Academy to learn Italian. In fact, she hadn't signed up at all. She was there under false pretenses. Expressly to earn a BFA. And if becoming a Boyfriend-Forgetting Alpha meant getting a detention or two in the process, so be it.

"So about the song." Darwin reached for his guitar. "Can I play what I have?"

"Sure." Allie politely reached for a link of wheat-meat. Was it supposed to be gray?

He tapped his hand on his faded jeans and began to hum. The beating of her heart matched his pace like a metronome.

When I met you I had fallen apart,
My insides on the outside, including my heart
But you listened to me and that slipped away,
You coated me in Teflon that magical day.

He stopped and looked at her expectantly.

Allie surreptitiously whipped the *blah*sage into the bushes and applauded. "Awesome. When did you write it?"

"Last night." He lowered his eyes shyly. "After you left."

Allie's stomach swooped and her lips tingled. Either the germs on her feet were seeping into her bloodstream or her crush was getting stronger.

"How's the cadence?" he asked. "Should I go for something faster?"

"Um, you could," Allie tried. "But, you know, is that what you're going for?"

Darwin stared at her, studying her face. Was he impressed with her feedback? Falling in love? Imagining what their kids would look like?

"Hmmmph," he grunted, his gaze holding steady.

This was it. The *I never thought I could feel this way about someone until I met you* moment.

"What?" Allie tucked her hair behind her ear and blinked her extra-long lashes at him. "Why are you looking at me like that?"

His lips curled into a frown. "I always thought your mole was on the left side."

Allie tasted a little bit of pancake in the back of her throat. Had she really been so stupid? She lifted a silver knife and checked her reflection. He was *right*. And so was the mole!

Allie rubbed the eyeliner away. "Is this what you're talking about?" She held out her thumb.

He nodded, looking adorably confused.

"Oh, that's just a makeup smudge. I was helping one of the girls get ready this morning." Her ears were ringing so loudly she could barely hear herself lie.

"Then where's your mole?"

"Oh, I um, I put concealer on it." She lifted her elbows to air out her pits. But the humidity was increasing by the second. The only wind came from her mouth.

"Why?"

"I didn't want people to know who I was, you know, in class. I want to be treated fairly. Judged like the other students."

He nodded, considering this. She could almost feel the grass growing beneath her fingers as she waited for Darwin's reaction. She plucked at the spongy tips nervously. What if didn't buy it? What if he realized it wasn't just the mole that was fake, but that she was, too?

"Admirable, but not necessary," he finally told her. "Everyone here is pretty incredible at what they do. You should own who you are. No hiding."

Allie grinned. If only he knew how right he was.

"Yeah, I guess that makes sense."

He popped a cinnamon-scented toothpick into his mouth and returned to his strings. "So, back to the cadence. You're saying leave it?" He strummed more forcefully than before.

"Darwin, shhhh," Allie pleaded. "Someone might hear you."

"Who? Everyone's at breakfast."

There was a rustle in the bushes and then the sound of footsteps coming toward them.

"Not *everyone*," said a familiar voice.

Allie gasped.

But for some odd reason, Darwin gasped louder.

10

Charlie opened the front door to Jackie O and let it slam behind her. Why had she hesitated back in Shira's office? Her roommates treated her like she was more invisible than an extra on *Perfect Storm*. Who was she trying to protect?

Starting up the winding glass stairs, Charlie's aPod sounded from inside her pocket. Four gold text bubbles stared back at her.

Taz: broke my arm this a.m., But at least I didn't break my bro's heart.

Melbourne: Your children would have been nearly as beautiful as me.

Sydney: How could you do this to us?

Dingo: You have been dingoed for the last time!

Charlie sniffled and selected a fresh uniform from her closet. There was a time when she would have given anything not to be Dingoed anymore. His pranks had gotten increasingly bigger-budget, more elaborate, and more dangerous. But now she missed the boys like a soldier misses his gangrenous foot.

Charlie leaned down and strapped on her clear gladiator sandals. She had just fastened the last strap when a song Darwin had been composing popped into her head. Singing along with the memory, she wished he knew how much she missed him. Longed to tell him she had done it for them, for their future. Hoped she'd prove herself to Shira soon, so she *could* tell him.

She hummed for another moment or two before realizing that the tune wasn't in her head. It was outside the house. And that could only mean one thing: Darwin was trying to win her back!

Charlie raced down the corkscrew staircase and bolted for the door. Technically, she wasn't allowed to *tell* Darwin. But maybe she could explain everything by *spelling* it with twigs and leaves. Or speak in clicks like the Bushmen they'd befriended in Tanzania. If Shira was going to play dirty, so could she.

Bursting outside, Charlie found her legs outrunning

her level head. She followed the music to the side of the house, and when she couldn't contain herself any longer she blurted, "Darwin, I'm so ha—"

Her voice trailed off as soon as she saw that a girl was sitting behind him on the blanket. He wasn't singing his way back to Charlie. He was replacing her—at her own picnic.

"Darwin, shhhh," Allie was pleading. "Someone might hear you."

"Who? Everyone's at breakfast."

"Not everyone," Charlie said flatly.

Darwin gasped, his face funneling through hurt, confusion, and guilt before landing on triumph. He had already moved on.

For a moment, the only sound in the garden was the fizzing glass of bubbles and pomegranate-extract on the blanket, Darwin's favorite breakfast concoction. The silence hurt more than a pimple, but Charlie couldn't bring herself to pop it.

Allie J's eyes flitted between the two of them, as if trying to decipher one of those optical illusion pictures that, after a stare-down, reveal a hidden image. Or in this case, a clear one.

"What are you doing here?" Darwin hugged his guitar like it was his best and only friend.

"I *live* here," Charlie snapped. She had never taken

him for the kind of guy who would try to make her jealous.

"You know each other?" Allie J asked. Her mole seemed to be missing, but Charlie couldn't be sure. Anxiety often blurred her vision.

"This is the ex," Darwin explained, a hint of shame in his voice.

Hearing him say the words made their breakup painfully real in a no-turning-back sort of way. She wasn't even *his* ex anymore. Just *the* ex, drained of any personal meaning.

"Brown-nose?" Allie J sounded genuinely shocked. "Darwin, *that's* who you were so up—" She stopped and changed course. "You dated *her?*"

"Why is that so surprising?" Charlie snapped.

"Who cares?" Darwin began packing the uneaten food. "It's over now."

"Clearly," Charlie's voice trembled.

"What was he supposed to do?" Allie J butted in. "Suffer? Just sit around and mope while you move on with your life?" Her voice began to tremble too, as if a fresh wound was talking for her.

Yes! Charlie wanted to answer. Darwin was *supposed* to be in mourning, just as she was, his heart cryogenically frozen the moment it broke, waiting for Charlie's return so it could thaw. Of course, he had no idea that she'd done it in order to ultimately keep them together. But shouldn't their history guarantee a future, even if the present sucked? Feelings didn't turn on and off like aPods or transfer over like frequent-flier miles—even when the first-class upgrade came in the form of Allie J.

"She's right." Darwin sided with Allie J. "You dumped me. On *Skype!*"

"Maybe she just wasn't that into you?" Allie J joked.

No one laughed.

Two quails scuttled across the yard, like a giddy couple on their first date. Charlie willed Darwin to put the pieces together. Her mom's speedy exit. The boy ban. Her sudden admittance. But he just stood there, looking at Allie J like she was a Brita pitcher—taking in all the negative and pouring out purity and rainbows.

"I better head to class." Darwin stood.

"Same." Charlie's eyes clouded with a 100 percent chance of rain. She turned and ran inside Jackie O without another word.

There was only one thing left to say. But not to Allie J or Darwin.

To Shira.

After the first tear fell, Charlie grabbed her aPod and typed a name. Turned out snitching was easier than she'd thought.

11

THEATER OF DIONYSUS
HONE IT: FOR DANCERS
MONDAY, SEPTEMBER 6TH
10:11 A.M.

Skye stretched her hammys while gazing up at the soaring glass box in front of her. The dance studio had windows where mirrors should have been and a glass floor instead of gleaming cherrywood. A girl with strawberry blond waves skirted around Skye and zipped into the elevator, but Skye paused outside for another moment. Straightening her lavender mesh sleeves, she tilted her face up to the sun. The air smelled of honeysuckle and promise.

"Wait for me!" a girl with two thick black braids woven with gold ribbon called from behind Skye. Skye recalled pooh-poohing the accessory when she was virtual shopping. Big mistake. Those strings had potential!

"I like your sleeves," said Gold String as they stepped inside the all-glass elevator. Her bright smile carved dimples in her cheeks.

"Thanks." Skye beamed, forgetting all about her accessory-envy. "They're kinda my thing."

"Truly inspired." The girl ran a tanned finger along the seam as if petting a furry caterpillar. "I'm Ophelia. I live in Angelina Jolie."

Skye introduced herself as the elevator shot them to the top floor with a minor jerk. They giggled nervously as the campus grew smaller and smaller below them. From up here, Skye could see the outline of the @-shaped island, the tram tracks that circled it, the glass-and-steel buildings growing out of the tropical foliage below, and the Mojave Desert in the distance.

When they reached the top, five other girls in various, albeit boring, interpretations of the uniform were scattered about the all-glass studio. Skye grinned. Plain dressers were plain people. And plain people had no passion. And dancers without passion were like writers without ideas or actors without issues.

Triple Threat stretched at the barre. "Heard from the boys?" she whispered.

"Yup," Skye replied faux-modestly, pulling her ankle to her butt. Not that she needed to warm up. She'd been born hot.

Triple nod-approved. "Mel texted me, but Renee said I should wait at least one hundred thirty-nine minutes before texting back."

"A hundred thirty-nine minutes?" Skye repeated.

"That's three episodes' time," Triple explained, retying her dance shoe. "Something to do with suspense and drama. Apparently three-episode arcs always leave people wanting more."

A ripple of annoyance crawled up Skye's spine. Who'd died and made Renee the boy whisperer?

Triple Threat fell gracefully over her legs. "You're lucky Mimi isn't here yet." She leaned sideways and grabbed her heel. "You're late."

"And you're lame," Skye shot back hastily, even though the comeback wasn't her best.

"Are you just going to stand there picking your sleeves?" Triple jutted one hip out.

The others, backlit by the blazing sun, tittered into their various body parts.

"Are you just going to stand there picking fights?" Skye countered.

"Silence!" snapped a statuesque woman. Her caramel-colored skin was so perfect it seemed airbrushed. With cat-like grace she padded to the front of the studio, the shapely results of decades of dance undulating under her bronze Lycra dress. "If you want to fight in my classroom, I'm all for it. But use your bodies, not your mouths. I don't ever want to hear what you have to say again. I only want to see it."

Triple lowered her leg from the barre and pliéd her respect.

Skye stood even straighter. A moment of self-loathing gripped her like toe shoes. The single-named legend had been her mother's idol for years.

"I'm sure you've noticed this is not your average dance studio." Everyone nodded in agreement. "You can be seen from all over campus." She gestured to the window-walls. "If you miss a step, everyone will see. Just like onstage. Understood?" She lifted her palm in a swooping motion.

The girls assumed first position.

"Now show me why Shira picked you. Music: On," Mimi ordered. "Instrumental. Minor-key tonality. Bass-centric." The room's hidden speakers responded to her voice command. A hip-hop beat thundered from the floor up. "Watch first. Ah-five-ah-six-ah-sev-un . . . eight." Mimi unfolded like a flower as she demonstrated an intricate routine made up of soutenus, stag leaps, and pencil turns. Skye burned the steps to memory, leaving room for a few tricks of her own. Challenging? Yes. Too challenging? Never.

"This time without me," she panted. "Re-cue music. Ah-five-ah-six-ah-sev-un . . . eight."

Skye tuned out the others and replicated every soutenu, stag leap, and pencil turn with remarkable accuracy. Then she added some sizzle to the steak with a few snaps and switches. She didn't need mirrors to tell her she was on. The crowd gathering below the studio was all the reassurance she needed.

Mimi wove through the dancers and stopped alongside Skye, who extended her arms farther, ready to catch the instructor's praise.

"Music off!" Mimi shouted, taking her place at the front of the studio. "Playback Skye."

At Mimi's command, a hologram of Skye appeared, her digital smile confident. All the girls *awww*ed in amazement at the projection. Skye shifted her feet to first position. It was a little early to be casting her as the one to watch, but not the least bit surprising. Jealousy-glares warmed her like a spotlight.

"Music. Dance." The faux Skye launched into the routine, and the real Skye's eyes widened in amazement. So *that* was why there were no mirrors. Why settle for 2-D when you could watch your hologram execute a perfect piqué in every possible dimension?

Skye squeaked with joy. Her routine was more stunning than she'd thought. Ending her drop-and-recover with a head snap was brilliant. Funny how the dramatic could become exquisite with a few simple tweaks.

When virtual Skye vanished, Mimi crossed her lithe arms over her ribby bird chest. "Thoughts? Ophelia, please begin."

"Good turnout?" She tugged nervously on one of her braids.

"Yes. In general, her form is decent."

Decent? *Decent* was how her father described the mileage on his new Audi.

"What about her style?" Mimi gazed at her pupils. "Andrea?"

Triple bristled at the sound of her real name. "Cheap."

A few of the girls giggled.

"I was referring to her *dance* style."

More giggles.

"Which was wonderful . . ."

Skye beamed.

". . . if she were dancing for a crowd of tourists in Times Square subway station, or perhaps the overly appreciative residents of a senior center. But highly inappropriate for a professional hired to execute a routine with perfection."

Humiliation tingles stung Skye's skin, and no one dared laugh this time. "I was just trying to—"

"To what?" Mimi barked, a faint trace of her Eastern European accent escaping. "To distract us with your flashy wrist warmers?"

"*Distract?*" Skye's ears began to ring. She felt like she was shrinking more than her fading hologram. If only . . .

"You're here to dance, not play dress-up, so lose the sleeves." Mimi's voice took on a hard edge. "Besides they're in violation of the uniform code."

Lose the sleeves! The words ricocheted through Skye's body and stabbed her in the heart. Fighting tears, she peeled them off slowly. Her arms felt naked and exposed. Her identity stripped.

Mimi held out her hand like a gum-hating teacher. Skye released the sleeves sadly.

"Let's go again. Follow the routine, not your impulses. Music on. Ah-five-ah-six-ah-sev-uhn, eight."

Skye began, but could feel herself a split second behind everyone else. A Rorschach pattern of sweat spread under her arms.

With an exasperated sigh, Mimi stopped the music again. "I guess it wasn't the sleeves causing the drag."

Skye's lips began to twitch. Why was Mimi picking on *her*?

"No sulking. Don't think. Feeeeel. Keep dancing . . . Andrea, promising lines. Soften your face . . . Prue, more hips, less lips . . . Ophelia, neutral spine . . . Less butt, Lacey! In fact, all of you can use less butt. I can't see your muscles with all of that flesh." Mimi curtsied, swung a gold tote over her shoulder, and exited without another word. "Practice on your own, girls. If you need to work through lunch, so be it."

For the first few seconds, no one spoke. A volatile dance teacher, no lunch, and the possibility that they were fat were a lot to process.

Finally, Ophelia broke the silence. She pinched a leg warmer, showed it to Skye, and whispered, "It could have been me."

Skye smiled appreciatively and then noticed her sleeves hanging over the barre. Lifeless and empty, they looked like anorexic sock puppets.

"Lunch will commence in five minutes," announced the Brit through the speakers overhead.

"We better go, Triple," Skye said to the campus below as it filled with alphas on their way to the Pavilion.

"Go where?" Triple released her bun. Her hair fell like a velvet curtain.

"The spa," Skye said with lots of *duh*. "The Jackie O's are scheduled for welcome treatments at noon today, hel-loooooo?" She leaned forward and whispered: "Our lunch will be served there, remember?" Skye winked at their good fortune, but Triple still looked confused. "Thalia told us about the change during breakfast."

"Oh yeah." Triple's light brown eyes flickered like a faulty lightbulb. Then she shrugged. "Oh well."

"Whaddaya mean?"

"We obviously can't go." She air-swept her arm like she was about to plié. "Look around. Everyone is practicing." Triple brought the hand back to her hip. "And it seems like you need all the practice you can get."

"Opposite. I over-delivered." Skye narrowed her turquoise eyes.

"Can you lead us in a routine, Triple Threat?" Prue called from across the room. The girls were forming a line. All they needed was a leader. The others nodded. Those nods looked familiar. They used to belong to Skye.

It was more painful than tendonitis.

"I'm outta here." Skye turned on her heel.

"Where are you going?" Ophelia called from her place in line.

"The spa."

"What about practice?" Lacey asked, her giant head and small body reminding Skye of Tweety Bird.

"I'm gonna loosen up at the spa instead. We're all probably a little stiff from our flights yesterday."

Ophelia, Lacey, and Sadie exchanged glances.

Skye squinted, noticing their potential interest. "Wanna come with me?"

"They can't!" Triple shouted.

"Why?" Skye kept her cool. "No one will know they're gone."

The girls nodded enthusiastically.

"Mimi will!" Prue insisted.

"Are you gonna tell her?" Ophelia butted in.

"No. I wouldn't do that. But she'll find out."

"Hey." Tweety leapt through the air. "Aren't we supposed to be fighting with our bodies?"

Skye and Ophelia cracked up.

"I'm in," Ophelia announced.

"Me too," chirped Tweety, landing.

"You're taking a big chance," Triple warned.

"You dance it and we'll chance it." Skye smirked.

Ophelia and Tweety grabbed their bags and followed Skye out of the studio. They weren't copying her moves yet—but at least they were following.

12

"All aPods must be powered down during your spa visit. Namaste," a recording of Bee's voice said when her daughter arrived in waiting room. As always, Charlie did what her mother asked and powered off.

"Thank you," the recording said.

Waiting for the others, Charlie sat surrounded by a representation of Australia's Great Barrier Reef, feeling more sunken than the layers of coral beneath her gladiators. Nudibranches, sea anemones, clown fish, sea turtles, and hundreds of other psychedelic-colored creatures lived under the glass floor and behind the walls. The sounds of lapping waves surrounded Charlie, making her seasick. The coconut-scented air did nothing to settle her roiling stomach. Old memories of Darwin on the beach mixed with new ones of him and Allie J couldn't be exhaled away. Amnesia was the only cure.

Suddenly her aPod beeped. Strange. She could have sworn she turned it off.

SHIRA: TICK . . . TICK . . . TICK . . . IT'S AL-MOST NOON!

Charlie thought about how she'd typed Allie J's name into her aPod earlier that morning but hadn't pressed send. She wondered why, but knew it had nothing to do with morality. So she'd snitch a little. Big deal. If it meant help-ing Shira break up Darwin and Allie J, it would be totally worth it. But what if she didn't? What if Shira was happy about their coupling? What if she approved? That would sting more than the jellyfish on the other side of the glass. And Charlie was already in enough pain.

Gripping her bracelets, she lowered her head between her legs and sighed. How could he have replaced her so quickly? A sand-colored crab fixed its beady black eyes on her as if to say he understood. Shira had probably separated him from someone special too.

"All aPods must be powered down during your spa visit. Namaste." Bee's voice sounded again.

"Well, look who's here. . . ."

Charlie didn't have to look up from the sea floor to know the voice belonged to Allie J.

"If you're auditioning for the part of Mean Girl Number

133

One, you've got the part," Charlie said, meeting Allie J's eyes. Allie J's sun-kissed skin glowed even more than usual.

That used to be *Charlie's* Darwin-induced glow.

"And you seemed to have snagged the role of Big Fat Liar," Allie J shot back. "Why would you lie about knowing the Brazille boys?" she asked, a combination of anger and awe in her voice.

But before Charlie could answer, Bee's voice filtered through the invisible speakers. "All aPods must be powered down during your spa visit. Namaste."

"Ohmuhgud!" someone gasped from just outside the spa. "Are we really underwater?"

Awe-filled giggles followed, and then Skye entered with two girls—obviously dancers. Who else would walk like a duck with back pain?

"All aPods must be powered down during your spa visit. Namaste." Even Bee's recording was beginning to sound tired as it repeated for the fourth time.

Renee appeared next, her pink hair teased to soap-opera proportions.

After a round of introductions, and a bunch of "I love your music"s, the girls glanced around the spa *ooh*ing and *ahh*ing. Charlie felt a bubble of satisfaction at having already previewed what the others were experiencing. But a second glance at the girls' spa blushes caused a jealousy-twinge at not being able to share in the moment. It was yet another thing that separated her from them.

"How incredible is this place?" Ophelia touched the wall, scaring a school of spiny lion fish into a frenzied about-face. "It's like we're inside a fish tank."

"Actually, it's the Great Barrier Reef," Charlie mumbled flatly.

"Meet Charlie Brown-nose." Skye shifted her feet from first to third position. "She memorized the Alpha Academy handbook."

"That's not the only reason she knows everything." Allie J pinched a handful of protein pellets from the spa bar and dropped them in her mouth.

Charlie stiffened. *Don't tell them . . . don't tell them . . . don't tell them. . . .*

"Aha!" Renee pointed at Charlie like a TV detective who'd caught her perp red-handed. "I knew there was more to this story."

The wave sounds picked up force.

"Please remove your uniforms and prepare to board your spa chair," said Bee's voice.

Just then, white canvas tubes lowered from above and covered each girl while she undressed. The timing was perfect. The cover gave Charlie's tears a chance to fall undetected. The front of the tubes opened suddenly, allowing each girl to board her conveyor table in privacy.

"Lie on your belly with your face in the cradle," Bee explained, "and prepare to be renewed from head to toe."

"I miss you, Mom," Charlie whispered as she wiggled under the warmed blankets and settled onto the padded table. The tubes lifted away, revealing a snaking conveyor belt that hauled massage tables like train cars. The lights dimmed, the fish glowed, and the girls began moving through the reef.

"So, guess who used to be Darwin's girlfriend?" Allie J mumble-shouted from her face cradle.

"Allie J, don't!" Charlie lifted her head, but a soft electronic hand pressed it back down and began kneading her shoulders. What would otherwise have felt relaxing became a lavender-scented straitjacket.

"Who?" Skye called from the back of the massage train.

"Brown-nose!" Allie J managed in spite of the smoldering hot rocks that were now being placed along their spines.

"Aha!" Renee bucked, knocking a stone to the ground. "That explains *everything*!"

"What?" Charlie barked, feeling defensive. "What does that *explain*?"

"It explains how you got into the academy," Allie J insisted.

Charlie's insides lurched as her secret leaked out like the pulsating stream of hot oil beating down on their backs.

"It explains why Darwin is so happy to be single," Skye shouted over the vibrating head massager.

"H-h-he sa-a-id that?" Charlie snapped, her voice trembling from the head massager. Or was it the news?

"He didn't have to," Skye insisted. "It was obvious by the way he looked at Allie J."

All of a sudden the chairs flipped over. Blasts of steam opened the pores on the girls' faces while a giant loofah exfoliated their bodies.

"Ahhhhhhh!" the girls shouted, half-laughing.

Allie J giggled as the exfoliator made its way down to their feet. "Ohhhh, this thing tickles." She giggled some more. "Do you think it's sanitary?"

"You're all wrong," Renee announced as the exfoliator stopped to switch sides. "It explains why we almost got busted visiting the boys last night!"

"You visited the boys?" Ophelia called from the back.

"The Brazille boys?" Lacey echoed.

"How do me and Darwin have anything to do with you almost getting busted?" Charlie pressed.

The exfoliator lowered again, rubbing away at their dead skin. The giggle-screaming resumed as the loofah zzzzzzzzzzzzed over their bodies.

"Because you told Shira we snuck out. That's why she sent that warning!" Renee declared loudly. "I've done enough espionage plots to know a traitor."

Like a tea bag in hot water, the accusation took a minute to steep before Charlie got its full flavor. But instead of feeling the sting of tears, she felt a surge of power.

From the safety of her white changing tube, she reached for her aPod and sent Shira the name. Her choice was clear.

SHIRA: THAT WASN'T SO HARD, WAS IT?

Charlie: Not at all.

SHIRA: NEXT TIME, DON'T BE LATE.

Charlie nearly dropped her aPod. *Next time?*

13

NORTH SHORE
THE JUNGLE
MONDAY, SEPTEMBER 6TH
2:15 P.M.

Allie tiptoed across the dirt (*ew!*) path and stopped by the monstrous tree at the end. Here on the north side of the island, the air was thick with moisture and smelled like earth, leaves, and bark. Memories of the Rainforest Cafe—or rather, the burger, fries, and sparkling volcano dessert—made her stomach grumble. Memories of Fletcher asking the waiter for two spoons made her heart ache.

From the base of the thick tree, Allie checked her schedule for the third time. Nothing had changed. Hone It: For Writers was located in the Fuselage. And the Alphas Positioning System, a.k.a. APS, on her aPod was flashing. Apparently she was there.

Seeing no other option, Allie began climbing spiral stairs that had been carved into the tree's trunk, praying with every step that fungus was not hyper-breeding in the humidity and taking root between her toes.

When she got near the top, she began to hear voices. She stopped on what felt like the eightieth step and quickly Purelled her feet. The robo-pedi, with all its exfoliating and scraping, had removed any natural germ shield she had formed, leaving her more vulnerable than ever. And she was *over* feeling vulnerable.

The stairs stopped at a tree house–type deck outfitted with a hammock, a telescope, and several pine-green couches. Attached to the deck was the Fuselage—a silver Boeing 747 that had been converted into a modern classroom. *SOAR* was written across the side in silver glitter script.

Eight airplane seats had been arranged in a circle in the center of the cabin. Three were free; girls pulling tray tables from their armrests filled the others. Once unfolded, Allie realized the "tray holders" were actually futuristic writing tablets, their gray screens hungrily awaiting strokes of brilliance. Grass covered the floor, and the windows had been removed to allow a warm breeze to circulate like whispered gossip.

"What is this place?"

"Cool, right?" answered a girl with a scratchy voice. She had dark hair, dark nails, a sapphire nose-stud, and an O-shaped mouth candied with matte red lipstick.

Something flickered out of the corner of her eye. Allie quickly claimed the empty seat beside Scratchy Voice, fearing spontaneous liftoff.

A 3-D wintry forest scene filled the cabin.

Everyone *oooooh*ed in awe.

Then the image morphed into a colorful tea party with a little scone that said *eat me*. Allie was tempted to do just that, since she had metabolized her vegan lunch during the tree-climb. She reached for it, but a glittering dining hall with floating candelabras replaced the virtual carb, which quickly became a closet door that opened into a sunlit field.

"Brilliant!" Scratchy applauded. She smelled like black coffee.

"What was that?" Allie asked, wishing she had something more meaningful to add.

"Sherwood Forest from *Robin Hood*. *Alice in Wonderland*'s tea party. The Hogwarts dining hall. The wardrobe from *Narnia* . . ."

"Oh, right," Allie said faintly. "Love those movies."

"Movies?" The girl sat back in disdain. "Please tell me you're joking."

"Why would I be joking?" Allie tried. "They were great. Just the other night I watched—"

"*Watched?*" Scratchy screeched. Her voice sounded like a zipper unzipping. "Those scenes are from naw-vels." She exhaled sharply. "They aren't meant to be *watched*. Why not have Hollywood chew your food for you too? Or pump your blood? Or cast your friends like some MTV reality—"

"That's enough, Hannah," a woman with short, uneven black bangs and a choppy chin-length bob insisted. Her narrow blue eyes were free of makeup but full of fire. "You can critique her writing, but not her lifestyle. Inspiration is all around us. Don't let the brain limit the mind."

"Sorry," Hannah said to the teacher and then held out her plump hand to Allie. "I'm Hannah."

"Hey." Allie shook then Purelled immediately.

"Better. And I'm Keifer Lutz." Keifer placed a fingernail-shaped thimble on her index finger and scribbled in the air. Her name appeared in 3-D letters on the oversize LCD blackboard at the front of the cabin. "I am here to blow dust off your talent and make it shine." She began handing out thimbles. "And you are here to dive into your hearts and expose your true selves. Like putting on an inside-out sock, you will need to dig deep and pull through."

Allie's stomach dipped. She felt like a sock, all right— dirty, full of holes, and stepped on. She immediately pulled out her aPod and scanned her teacher.

NAME: KEIFER LUTZ. BECAME A PUBLISHING PHENOM IN HER EARLY TWENTIES WITH HER FIRST NOVEL, *FIFTH AVENUE HAPPENSTANCE*. WITH COMPARISONS TO J. D. SALINGER, HARPER LEE, AND TRUMAN CAPOTE, SHE PROVED THAT A YOUNG VOICE CAN BE RELEVANT, DISARMING, AND BEAUTI- FUL. SPENT THE LAST NINE YEARS IN PARIS WRITING NINE-

TEEN INTERNATIONAL BEST-SELLERS AND TRANSLATING
THEM HERSELF INTO SIX LANGUAGES. PLANS ON LEARNING
SANSKRIT, HEBREW, AND CANTONESE DURING HER STAY AT
THE ACADEMY. IS CURRENTLY WORKING ON A BOOK ABOUT
FAILED POLITICAL LEADERS AND THE WOMEN WHO LOVED
THEM.

So far, impersonating Allie J had been as easy as quoting the odd lyric, concealing her natural beauty, and surviving without shoes. But surely a real writer would be able to see *impostor* bubble lettered between the lines of her first essay. And when Keifer discovered Allie had no clue how to write in one language, let alone six, she'd no longer be a sock. She'd be a bra—busted!

Charlie shuffled into the classroom and claimed the last seat. Her cheeks were still red from the spa. She took the seat across from Allie, offering a tight smile.

"What are you doing here?" Allie whispered while Keifer helped a girl with ringlets wrestle her tablet out of the armrest.

Charlie shrugged. "It was on my schedule. I don't have a set major."

"Yes, you do," she whispered loud enough for Hannah to hear. "Major pain in my butt."

Hannah rolled her no-sense-of-humor eyes. Charlie lowered her head, her long brown bangs concealing her sadness like tent flaps.

Allie pictured her alpha crush—sun-streaked hair, hazel eyes, freckle above his lip . . . How had Charlie ever gotten him? The same way Trina got Fletcher? Was it . . . *talent?* Hmmmm. Maybe, just like blind people sharpened their other four senses to survive, plain Janes developed other, non-beauty-related skills to attract boys. But what was Charlie's?

Allie pulled a handful of hair over her shoulder to check for splits (none) and ran her fingers over her poreless skin for blemishes (also none), reminding herself that as Allie J, she was the full package—beauty and brains. Her days of getting trumped by chumps were over.

A broad-shouldered boy eclipsed the thick band of light streaming through the doorway. His features were back-lit but his silhouette was unmistakable. "Darwin?" Allie J heard herself say.

Charlie followed Allie's gaze to the doorway. She swallowed hard, as if forcing back that barf urge that comes when your ex-boyfriend appears unexpectedly.

"Welcome," Keifer said, ignoring the hisses of plane seats as the girls shifted nervously on their perches. "Please tuck in your oxford, then take the seat beside Allie J."

Allie beamed like a raffle winner.

"You're *Allie J?*" Hannah whispered. "Wow! Hey, I didn't mean to harsh on you about the whole movie thing. Songwriting and novel writing are two totally different skills and—"

"Cool. No worries," Allie muttered as Darwin passed Charlie's chair. He slowed just a little, as if drawn in by an invisible force field. A force Allie prayed was fueled by the kind of emotion that makes you never want to get back together with someone.

Finally Darwin settled into the empty seat next to Allie. His eyes crinkled hello.

"Everyone's here, so let's begin." Keifer claimed the center of the circle, her bangs more crooked than Tori Spelling's boobs. "Two rules. One: No hand-raising in my class. I'll either call on you, or you'll just speak up. Rule number two: Call me Keifer. Rule number three: No flirting."

More of the girls giggled awkwardly. Charlie stared at the grass floor.

"Sounds good, Keifer," Hannah blurted.

Allie and Darwin exchanged an eye roll. She felt a spark all the way down to her muddy toes.

Keifer smiled at her new pet, then pressed a button on her aPod. The roof retracted, giving way to the bright, cloud-streaked sky. "The Fuselage is symbolic of your upcoming journey. There is no limit to where your imagination can fly."

The girls lifted their eyes and peered out at the endless possibilities. Allie mostly saw a whole lot of blue sky.

"Faulkner, Dickens, Angelou, Rowling, me . . . You have the potential to be as good as these greats. And do you know why?"

Hannah raised her hand. Keifer shook her head disapprovingly.

"Because you're all starting from the same place." She touched her heart with one hand and pointed to their tablets with the other. "The need to express yourself, and a blank page."

Suddenly, Allie was overcome with inspiration. She had suffered more than any of those so-called writers and experienced more sadness in the last month then they had in a lifetime. So why not share it with the world? Give the people someone real to relate to. Someone other than Oprah. Allie's innards jumped. Her soul was rising to the occasion.

"This page is a time machine, a teleporter, a magic wand. With it you can create a world. Give life. Take it away. Then resurrect it. But it only works with honesty and specificity, and it all starts here." She wiggled her thimble-clad finger. "You have fifteen minutes. Give me a paragraph on what you're feeling *right now*. One caveat: Don't overthink it. In fact, don't think at all. Let your heart do the writing. Begin."

Allie froze, her soul-jumping inspiration congealing like old sweet 'n' sour sauce.

Darwin lowered his head and began scribbling. Allie tried peeking, but his upper body hung half-moon over his tablet.

Allie summoned her sorrow. Fletcher, Trina, identity theft—emotions began to rise again, but stopped just before they reached her thimble finger. They were *feelings*, not sentences. It was pain, not words. It was a missive on hell, not a beach read.

But wait! This paragraph wasn't about *her*. It was about Allie J. The girl who rebounded from breakups like a rubber pinball. So all Allie A had to do was funnel her words through Allie J's industrial-strength heart and—

"Fingers down."

"Serious-leh? That was fifteen minutes?" Allie looked around, but no one else seemed surprised.

"It sure was." Hannah beamed.

"Hannah, why don't you go first." Keifer brushed a choppy layer behind her heavily pierced ear.

"Sure." She cleared her throat and looked around meaningfully at each of her classmates. "I am here because I killed an American girl."

The entire class gasped. Hannah's lips curled in a smug smile and began to read. "'When I was five, I killed my American Girl doll.'"

Everyone giggled with relief except Darwin, whose Y chromosomes prevented him from understanding the sanctity of the plastic childhood treasure. "'She came with this prefab story of how she'd survived the Depression. But I found the idea of breadlines boring, so I wrote my own. She was the star of my first play, *The Case of the Doll Murder*. At the end, Barney the Dinosaur, played by my reluctant younger brother, was carted away as the culprit. Miraculously, the doll was revived after a posthumous surgery by a GI Joe medic. But the damage was done. I'd been bitten by the writing bug, and I never recovered.'"

Keifer gave an appreciative smile, which granted the rest of the class permission to applaud. "The moment of recognition for a young writer. Charming. Now let's see it."

The 3-D images on the wall returned. This time they contained the bare outlines of a dinosaur, a solider, and a large-headed doll.

"Shira has created Wordz-to-Life software," Keifer explained. "This program allows us to *watch* your stories, and help you see where you need more detail."

"Now, tell me what's wrong with this picture."

Hannah's lip stuck out and trembled a bit.

A girl with a short pixie cut and C-plus cups spoke up. Allie quickly scanned her.

NAME: YARA NEGRON, MICHELLE OBAMA HOUSE. LIKES: SHAKESPEARE, BRITISH SLANG, AND WRITING MUSICALS. DISLIKES: LLAMAS, ANGLOPHILES, AND LICKING ENVELOPES.

"Hannah didn't *show* us the scene," Yara said. "She just told it to us. I didn't feel like I was living it with her. So I had no connection to it."

"Bridgette Wu from Heidi Klum," another girl said, tossing a slick black braid over her shoulder. "She expected us to bring our own vision to fill in the drama. I think that's cool. Very minimalist. Smacks of Dingo."

"Your brother's a writer too?" Allie whispered to Darwin.

Darwin laughed like she was joking.

"Disagree," Ringlets, aka Tatiana, insisted. "Keifer wanted *us* to create the story. And that's not our job as readers. It's hers as the writer."

"Lazy!" coughed Yara.

Tatiana giggled.

Hannah hung her head.

"I agree." Keifer nodded. "It is lazy. But chin up, Hannah. You're great at coming up with brilliant ideas. You wouldn't have created three successful novel franchises if you weren't. This is why we're here. To learn how to write visually. You gave people the bones. Now it's time to flesh them out and bring them to life."

Hannah scribbled notes—*lazy . . . chin up . . . bones . . . flesh out*—over her tablet. They appeared in Times New Roman font. She reduced the font size to 8-point the second she caught Allie peeking.

"Charlie, you're next."

Please make Charlie suck, please make Charlie suck, please make Charlie suck, Allie begged the clouds above. Still and serene, they offered no guarantee.

"'For the first time in my life, I am alone.'" Her voice was small and shaky. "'I walk around this palace of glass that, in defiance of gravity and zoning regulations, rises up and pierces the sky. The hovercraft technology, the holographs that look friends but fade like jeans, feel like something I dreamed up.'" Her voice grew stronger, more confident. "'But it's all real, and I'm here to experience it—by myself. I'm walking down a red carpet with no escort, singing praises into the wind, and writing a story no one will read. As I walk and talk and sit and breathe, I want you with me, your arm linked through mine. . . .'"

Allie's fingers tightened around her Purell. Was Charlie trying to make up with Darwin in front of all these people? Was he falling for it? She didn't dare look. She didn't want to know.

"'But it's time for me to do it on my own. Your absence was the price of admission. Still, I miss you. . . .'" Her voice trailed like a passing car. She swallowed hard as if bracing herself. "'I miss you, Mom,'" Charlie finished.

Allie sighed. Darwin ran a hand through his hair and slouched.

"Very evocative, Charlie," Keifer said. "Now let's see it."

The walls went blank. A faceless girl walked through a foggy space alone. Futuristic buildings rose up around her, making her appear smaller and smaller as her journey continued. A blurry figure appeared, and the faceless girl chased after it. It came a little more into focus and then faded away, leaving the girl alone in the fog forever.

"Any thoughts on Charlotte's piece?" Keifer prompted.

Allie could feel Darwin tense beside her.

"She gave us a window inside what it is to be alpha, which often means sacrifice," tweeted a sunburned girl with blond eyebrows.

Tatiana spoke next. "Um, you know, at first, knowing it was going to be posted on-screen, I felt like the piece would suffer because of the lack of description. But instead of painting a portrait of her surroundings, she painted her feelings. And that came through. It rang true. I really felt her longing."

Darwin looked at Charlie for a charged beat and then sat tall. "I thought it was confusing. No, *deceptive*." He paused, as if allowing his words to sink in for full sting-effect. "It felt like one of those stupid stories that ends in a dream."

"Uh, are you saying *The Wizard of Oz* is stupid?" Tatiana twirled her nose ring in victory. "Because that ended in a dream, and it also happens to be an American classic."

Charlie smiled her thanks.

"No, not like that at all," Darwin countered. "More like the writer wanted you to believe one thing and then made it all pointless by saying it was another thing altogether."

"What did *you* believe?" Keifer asked, folding her arms across her white tunic and cocking her head.

"I dunno." Darwin shrugged. "I just thought it was about someone else."

"I agree with Tatiana." Keifer blinked. "Charlie, excellent work. Bailey and Tatiana, good critiques. Darwin, you need to expand your mind and open yourself up to the different ways of storytelling."

Charlie smirked.

"Darwin, why don't you go next?"

"Fine." He cleared his throat. "'It was the day after my apocalypse. My brothers were with me in the fallout shelter. Each took a different tactic. Melbourne was a mercenary. Sydney was sensitive. Dingo was ready to prank revenge. And Taz was ready to climb the Pavilion and shout at the top of his lungs. My brothers insisted the dawn would come—a dawn I believed was doomed. But they were right. There it was, bright and shining. I just had to open my eyes and look.'"

Darwin's story splashed around the room. Faceless boys were pacing around a sad-faced Darwin in the near dark. And then light rose around them. Darwin smiled. The light didn't have a face.

Allie suddenly wondered if it was her.

She side-glanced at Darwin, asking with her fake green eyes if she was the sunrise. He blinked back that she was.

Fletch never would have been that poetic. She wanted to reach out and kiss his adorable freckle. But she decided on a smile, which he immediately returned.

"Nice work, Darwin. A promising start."

"Thanks," Darwin mumbled modestly.

"Allie J, what have you got for us?" Keifer rubbed her hands together like she was about to dig into a steaming plate of cheese fries. "You aren't the only talent in the Fuselage, but you *are* the only celebrity. And I'm sure I speak for all of us when I say I am very anxious to hear your prose."

Everyone applauded—except Charlie.

Oh no. Allie began sweating. She couldn't read her piece. It wasn't ready. It wasn't written! "But class is over in, like, three minutes," she tried.

"Then I suggest you start now," Keifer insisted gently.

The writers' circle provided no place to hide. Allie cleared her throat nervously and began improvising, just like she had on her acting auditions back in the old days. The days before Fletcher and—

"Allie J?"

"Sorry. Okay. Um, here I go," she said to the blank tablet. "Love triangle. Obtuse, acute, where do I fit in?" She peered up. Everyone was watching her. Her mouth dried. "So, um, where was I? Oh yeah. Isosceles, equilateral, scalene. What's your angle? Love triangle." She giggled with pride at her accidental but fabulous rhyme. "I can't let her win. Love triangle. Obtuse, acute, where do I fit in? Love geometry. Never mind, I pick me. The heart."

There was silence when Allie looked up, indicating she was finished. Had she made them all speechless?

"Comments?" Keifer finally asked the room.

Hannah's brows shot up under her mess of dark hair. Charlie nibbled her unglossed lip. Yara wiggled her nose like she was trying to contain a sneeze—or a snicker. Darwin fidgeted in his chair. Allie tilted back her head, willing the blood to drain from her face and return it to its naturally un-red state.

"Okay, then, let's see it."

Allie watched in horror as a thin blue line drew an isosceles triangle. Then an equilateral and scalene. And then a heart.

Snickers peppered the existing tension.

Darwin shot Allie a pitying *what happened?* look. Somehow, Allie managed to shrug her shoulders, wondering if he'd buy stage fright.

"Catchy," Keifer finally spoke after a painfully long pause, "but I didn't want something I could dance to. Or trace for that matter." She cleared her throat, "I want something I can feeeeeel." Allie slid down in her chair as Keifer continued, wishing she could power up the jet and fly away from her classmates' accusing stares. "This is a poem, not a paragraph. I'd say there's a rhyming dictionary where your heart should be. And not that cutesy heart, either. The bloody one that pumps life into your body every single day."

"Class is dismissed," the British voice announced all across campus. Allie had no idea who that voice belonged to, but she wanted to send her a dozen roses and a crate of thank-you chocolates.

Keifer clapped. "Class, I want you to finish what we started here today. Add a hundred words and more description."

Everyone stood.

"Allie J, stay," Keifer demanded. Allie nodded for Darwin to go ahead, hoping he couldn't hear her heart beating triple time.

When everyone was gone, Keifer *a-hem*ed and handed Allie a piece of paper. "Sign this." OMG. Was she making her drop the class, leaving Charlie and Darwin together without her? "I'd like your autograph."

Relief washed over Allie like a tsunami. So her triangles weren't that bad! Maybe they were actually genius in their simplicity—like Post-its or Reese's Peanut Butter Cups. Keifer had probably just been hard on her so the others wouldn't feel badly about not being brilliant.

"Of course," Allie said with a smile. "Who should I make it out to?"

"Just sign it," Keifer ordered, handing her a pen.

Allie executed her perfectly practiced Allie J signature, dotting the J with a messy peace sign.

Keifer palmed the signed piece of paper, wadded it up, then tossed it in the recycling bin. "Now that we've thrown away the big star, we can get down to the real Allie J. I want to know what lies behind those green eyes. Somewhere inside you is a talented girl with something worth saying. Your songs are proof of that. And *that* is the girl I want in my class."

The branches over the Fuselage swayed in the light breeze, and the sun beat down on Allie's part. She nodded, her hope fading like her roots. Because underneath the fake mole, Allie was just a heartbroken blonde with no idea what to say.

14

APOD MESSAGE
TO ALL STUDENTS AND FACULTY
MONDAY, SEPTEMBER 6TH
6:19 P.M.

PLEASE REMAIN SEATED AFTER DINNER FOR THE
G'DAY ADDRESS. ATTENDANCE IS MANDATORY.

—SHIRA

15

The Pavilion was alive with the sound of gossip as one hundred girls sat around empty tables trying to guess the subject of Shira's g'day address. Rumors ranged from "She's opening an academy for boys" to "Shira is actually a famous Australian game show host in drag." Tired of useless theories, Skye was ready to focus her energy on something more productive. Like, why weren't the guys at dinner? Why hadn't she heard from Taz? Why . . .

Her aPod vibrated.

"Yes!" she blurted, then quickly lowered her voice and turned to Renee. "Taz just texted!" she whispered. Thalia was at the table with them, but Charlie Brown-nose concerned her more. Renee had been calling Charlie out as a spy all afternoon. And even though Skye believed Renee had SOS (Soap Opera Syndrome: confusion over where storylines in soap operas end and reality begins), why chance it?

"What did he say?"

"He wants to know when we can sneak out again." She waved her aPod as proof. "And I say the sooner the better. Before our spa glows fade." Skye stroked her cheek, marveling at how smooth it felt. "What good is beauty if it can't be admired by boys? It's like cutting the label out of a Chanel dress."

"Or marrying Spencer without the MTV cameras," Renee added.

"Exactly." Skye tossed her hair. "What's the point?" Without further hesitation, she texted back.

Skye: B there once r muse takes her snooze.

She was about to hit send when Renee smacked her. The aPod flew under the table.

"Are you crazy?" Skye narrowed her turquoise eyes.

"Relax," Renee insisted. "I know what I'm doing. And you can't send that text."

"Why?" Skye scanned the dining hall. Everyone was still seated at their six-leaf-clover tables chatting away. Triple was rolling her neck, making it clear she didn't care what they were talking about. And Charlie was talking to Thalia about some woman they knew named Bee. "No one's watching."

"What's going on?" Allie J leaned in expectantly.

"I got another message. They want to know when we're coming," Skye muttered.

"You have to wait one hundred and thirty-nine minutes," Renee told her.

"In bed!" Allie J cracked.

Renee rolled her eyes. "It's kind of confusing, but trust me—I know. Don't text yet."

"Triple already told me about your theory." Skye sat up a little straighter. "But I'm even better at boys than I am at dance. So don't tell me how to flirt and I won't tell you how to act."

"Have you seen Rayne Storm?" Triple chimed in with a provocative grin. "Maybe you *should* tell her how to act."

Skye instantly forgave Triple for her spa defection.

Renee's violet eyes darkened with rage. "Maybe you should tell yourself to shut—"

"G'day!" Shira's sharp accent hacked off the end of their conversation. The glass dome became silent.

She was rising from some mysterious place beneath the stage, wearing a tight black tube dress and an even tighter smile.

"Congratulations. You all survived your first day." She grin-paused for applause, then lifted her chin, nudging them back into silence. Skye's stomach lurched. "You all came to the island for one year of intensive training in your field of expertise. But I want to give you more than that."

A few girls applauded. Shira lifted her hand, and they stopped at mute-button speed.

"I have no doubt that you've spent many sleepless nights imagining yourselves dancing on the best stages, cooking for monarchs, accepting Oscars, and building a better tomorrow. I know this because I used to do the same. And I have since accomplished it all." Shira glided around the edge of the stage, making sure to connect with each girl as much as someone in dark sunglasses could. "So believe me when I say that I am here to make your daydreams come true. Not only while you're on my island, but while you are on my planet. When you graduate, I will put all of my resources—of which there are many—behind you. My power and your talent will ensure that you are the biggest contributors in your fields for the rest of your life. You have my word."

Everyone burst out of their seats, their excitement exploding off the Pavilion's glass walls like fireworks. Their futures were set. Their wishes granted. Fame and fortune guaranteed.

Amid the chaos, Skye crouched down to retrieve her aPod from under the table. Taz had texted again.

Taz: 11:30 observatory sounds kl. We can climb the dome and slide down. Mjr rush!

"Huh?" Skye said to the screen. "Who said anything about the observatory?"

"I did," Renee gloated as they took their seats. "Isn't it a great idea? Totally romantic."

"That was your idea?" Skye narrowed her turquoise eyes in confusion.

"Yup. I just sent it and he responded in like half a second. I mean, Sydney is cute and all, but Taz is so much fun . . ." Renee twirled a strand of pink hair around her finger. "I guess I know a thing or two about boys after all."

Skye's heart began punching her chest. Her ribs held it back like a bouncer. "What about your one-hundred-and-thirty-nine minute rule?"

"It's definitely been that long for me." Renee winked. *Gotcha.*

"Ohmuhgud, you're such a—"

"Shhhhhhhh." Thalia silenced them from the other end of the table with a butter-colored finger to her lips.

"But as I'm sure you all know . . ." Shira continued from her perch on stage. The last standers quickly took their seats. "There can only be *one* alpha."

Smiles dropped like stocks. Murmurs rose and morphed into grumbles. Skye strained, anticipating further explanation. But all she heard was blood pumping against her eardrums.

"Will Renee Foraday please stand up?" Shira pressed her hands together as if in prayer and tapped them against her lips.

"Me?" Renee gushed, obviously drawing from an old Emmy speech. "You pick me?"

Shira nodded yes. "I pick you."

This time the applause was sparing, like the last few snaps of popcorn in the microwave.

Renee's wet violet eyes met Skye's hard turquoise ones as she stood. She extended her arms for a hug but Skye remained seated, weighted down by a billion questions. Most of them starting with, *What about me?*

Allie J smiled in a good-sport kind of way. Triple Threat began shouting at Thalia about the unfair edge celebrities had over people with true talent. Charlie lowered her head into her hands. Skye felt uncomfortable, like she was trying to squeeze into toe shoes three sizes too small.

The roof retracted just enough to let the moonlight illuminate Renee as she stepped onto the stage. A guarantee from Shira and a kiss from the universe—what next? Her own handbag line?

Renee stopped beside Shira, then waved at the unlucky ninety-nine with no regard for their crushed dreams. No idea how cheated they felt. No clue that they wanted to scratch her eyes out.

"Renee, you are a stunning example of hubris," Shira began.

"Thank you," Renee mouthed, bowing her head in gratitude.

Shira pursed her lips. "The Greek word *hubris* refers to the excess of ego and pride that often leads to a hero's downfall. Hubris was the biggest sin in ancient times." Her voice hardened.

Every set of eyes in the room fixed on the alpha. It was quiet enough to hear a bobby pin drop. Renee's smile began to fade. Or was that the moon losing interest?

"And just as Hera and Athena punished the Greeks whose egos were outsize, I too will not tolerate hubris."

The moon faded even more.

"What did I do?" Renee pleaded, her body suddenly shrouded in darkness.

"You went to see my boys."

Skye's feet tingled. Ohmuhgud, was she going to be next?

"And, as I stated earlier, that is against the rules." A frosty breeze rushed inside the cracked ceiling, turning Shira's breath into a cloud of anger. "You are no longer welcome at Alpha Academy. Your muse has your luggage. Exit at once," she thundered.

Thalia appeared on stage with two rolly suitcases—Skye hadn't even noticed that she'd left the table—and guided her toward the exit. Renee struggled to escape Thalia's grip, but the tall, butter-colored muse held firm.

"I told you Charlie was a spy!" Renee managed to shout before one last tug from Thalia had her at the door. Renee's violet eyes welled and two rivers of mascara-infused tears trailed down her cheeks. "I told you alllll!"

The instant she was gone, Shira continued.

"From this moment on, I will banish students as I see fit. There are countless temptations in this world and they come in all forms. Hold on to yourself. Follow your dreams. Obey my rules. And you just might be the one to win it all. Good luck."

Shira sank back down through the opening in the stage, leaving ninety-nine girls in a state of complete shock. For a few moments everyone stayed put, as if glued to the Lucite seats. Then Oprah's muse stood and stewarded her girls to the exit. The spell was broken, and everyone filed out of the Pavilion in silence.

Skye carefully put one gladiator-sandaled foot in front of the other, walking two paces behind her remaining housemates. She'd always pushed the limits back in Westchester— there had been secret rooms used to spy on boys, country club break-ins, and a black-and-white roof party with all the boys' sports teams and just her four BFFs. But expulsion wasn't something that happened to girls like her. It happened to boys who smoked cigarettes and drew anatomically correct pictures of teachers. And if it *did* happen to her, she'd have to go home in ignominy, with all of Westchester knowing she wasn't really an alpha. The realization slammed into her with the force of a speeding

SUV: This place would end in tragedy to for all but one girl.

And Skye *had* to be that one. She wanted it—and her mother *expected* it.

The second she got back to Jackie O, Skye rushed upstairs to bury her true feelings in the one place no one would ever think to look: her lavender ballet shoe.

HAD No. 4: Stay on Charlie's good side.

HAD No. 5: Claim Renee's closet.

HAD No. 6: Be the alpha.

16

Later that night, Charlie slipped her nightgown over her head—an extra-long silver tee that grew or lost sleeves based on her body temp—and stared at herself in one of the floating bathroom mirrors. The same medium brown eyes stared back at her, but she didn't feel the same. In four short hours she'd gone from informant to assassin. And thanks to a lucky guess by Renee, everyone knew. Yesterday she'd been desperate for friends. Tonight she would have settled for eye contact.

A minty lump formed in the back of her throat. It tasted like toothpaste and guilt. She wouldn't miss Renee—or the name Charlie Brown-nose. But if she'd known that naming names would result in public expulsion, would she have chosen differently—or even at all?

In that instant, her resentment toward Shira quadrupled. She had given up her loved ones for the opportunity to be here. And for what?

From the safety of a stall, Charlie broke through the firewall and texted her mum for the fourth time that day.

Charlie: She expelled Renee. All my fault. If I'd known this was what she wanted me for, I never would have accepted. You'd still be here. I'd still be with Darwin.

Bee: And you'd be in New Jersey, not living up to your full potential.

Charlie: As a spy?

Bee: As an alpha.

Tears gathered behind Charlie's eyes. It felt like forever since anyone had said something nice to her.

Bee: Thought you were going to turn in the songwriter.

Charlie: Changed my mind. Long story.

How was she supposed to explain she loved Darwin too much to get rid of his new girlfriend? It sounded crazy. But she couldn't cause him any more pain than she already had. No matter how much it hurt to see him and

Allie J together. Besides, Renee had caught on to the spy thing. And Charlie had wanted to make sure she stayed quiet before she spread the word. A lot of good that had done.

Bee: I've got time.

More than anything, Charlie wanted to ask her mother why Shira had put her in the writing class in the first place. Was it simply an attempt to twist the knife she had already lodged in her heart? To punish her for a lifetime of adoring Darwin by forcing her to watch him with his new crush? Bee was the only one who understood Shira's mind. But Charlie didn't want to go there. Why make Bee worry about her daughter's happiness? She'd already sacrificed so much.

Charlie: It's OK. How r u?

Bee: Great! Got a job at channel 4 as a producer. Shira wrote me a brilliant rec. Sent her the coffee recipe as a thank-you.

Charlie: Congrats, mum! You deserve it. You've been producing Shira's life for years.

Bee: All 4 u.

Charlie: I hear your voice every day on the announcements. Makes me miss u more!

Bee: Miss you too! Night-night. Don't let the alphas bite.☺

Once she logged off, Charlie began sobbing. Even though she'd spent the majority of her life traveling to foreign and unfamiliar places, she'd never felt more lost. More uncertain of her role in the universe and less motivated to figure it out. Why bother? With no one to share it with, success would be just another reminder that she was alone.

After restoring the firewall and washing her face, Charlie pressed her forehead against the bathroom's frosted-glass wall. A day at Alpha Academy was beginning to feel like a season of *24*—how could so much happen in so little time?

Back in the bedroom, the girls were sharing moisturizer and playing *Survivor: Alpha Island Celebrity Edition*, a game to decide which famous women would make Shira's cut. They were clearly too afraid that the topic they really wanted to discuss—Renee's axing—might get them expelled too.

"Tyra?" Triple said, rubbing sage-scented cream into her bony elbows.

"Alpha," Allie J determined.

"Lauren Conrad?" Skye asked, twisting her blond waves into a high bun.

Allie J banged on her pillow like it was a buzzer. "Alpha!"

"You watch *The Hills?*" Triple lifted her arched brows in surprise.

"Um, only because they wanted to use one of my songs for the open. But I turned them down. Too superficial."

"Know your history, Allie J!" Skye admonished. "Didn't you watch *Laguna Beach?* Once a beta, always a beta. Vanessa Hudgens?"

"Not alpha," Triple insisted.

"How can you say that?" Allie J asked vehemently. "Record deal. Huge box office. And Zac?"

"You can't be alpha if your boyfriend is more famous than you," Triple *duh*ed, slamming the cap on the moisturizer as if her word was final.

Allie J turned to Charlie and smirked. "So true."

An invisible hand grabbed Charlie's heart and squeezed.

"See anything you'd like to report?" Allie J snapped.

Charlie lay down on her bed and looked up at the dome skylight overhead. The moon was a smile-shaped sliver, and a single star glowed beside it. She thought of Darwin's mouth and the freckle she had kissed so many times.

Allie J pointed at her wrist, where a watch should be. "We should get going."

"No way. Mission's off." Triple ran the leftover moisturizer through her nonexistent split ends.

"Why?" Allie J hissed through clenched teeth like a rookie ventriloquist. She was accessorizing her bedtime tank–boy shorts combo with a thin cotton scarf. She looked half rollergirl, half hipster.

"Were you not there when Renee got chopped?" Skye eased herself back against her pillows and eyed Charlie with a mix of thanks and respect. She patted the lavender shoe that hung from her lamp. For a moment she looked like she was homesick too.

Charlie smiled back shyly.

"Big picture, Allie J." Skye extended her graceful arms, palms up. "Boy you met yesterday." She raised her left hand to shoulder level. "Or dream you've had since you were in vitro."

Charlie snickered. *You mean in utero,* she wanted to say but didn't dare. Besides, she had respect for Skye and her newfound priorities. Charlie had never imagined the girl who used boys' lips to blot her lip gloss would lead the charge away from them. But here she was, holding Allie J back like a sports bra.

"Why can't we have both?" Allie J countered.

A nauseating wave of déjà vu flooded Charlie and she fell back against her comforter. After all, she'd just been confronted with the same choice yesterday and had regretted her decision ever since.

"Because *both* isn't an option right now, okay?" Skye

snapped. "We all have to make sacrifices for the things we want most. Believe me, I don't like it either." She switched off her light and turned onto her side.

Something about what Skye said must have resonated with Allie J too, because she released a defeated sigh and climbed into her bed. "I guess."

"Smart choice," Thalia called from downstairs. Charlie had forgotten about her exceptional hearing. "As the Dalai Lama says, 'Sleep is the best meditation.'" And with that, the overhead lights flicked off.

Charlie sighed with relief and climbed under her covers. One by one, the girls' breathing slowed and steadied. Skye released a purr-snore, and Triple covered herself to the eyebrows with her comforter.

Charlie flipped onto her side and saw two green catlike eyes glaring at her in the darkness.

"I'm watching you," Allie J whispered. And then she rolled over.

Charlie began to sweat, and her nightgown adjusted by auto-rolling up the sleeves and shortening the hem. The dwindling tank made her think of how she acted around Shira, shrinking into herself so she wouldn't get in the way.

Well, it was time for all that to change. Time to show Shira she was more than a spy for hire. Time to show her roommates she could be trusted. And time to show Darwin that she was doing it all for him.

17

The vibe at breakfast was more grave than a cemetery until Allie's aPod vibrated.

Darwin!

It had been well over ten hours since their last correspondence, and she'd been starting to wonder if getting her poetic license publicly suspended by Keifer had turned him off. Angling away from Thalia and her superhuman senses, she clicked to read. But it was simply another spy joke from "anonymous." Just like the ones before it.

Q: Why does Shira wear dark glasses?
A: She has Charlie for eyes.

A chorus of suppressed snickers followed. But Allie was the only one who dared peek at Charlie's reaction. Everyone else was too afraid of being Reneed.

Allie waited to see if Charlie would shovel down her eggs Benedict, like one of those remorseless characters on *The Sopranos* whose appetites were unaffected by their crimes. Instead she drew a sad face in the low-fat, protein-enriched hollandaise sauce pooling on her plate, then went Jackson Pollock on it with the prongs of her fork.

Allie sighed. Shira wasn't in the cafeteria in person, but she was there in weather. Fat raindrops pelted the glass dome, each loud splat sounding like the blade of a guillotine drop-slicing someone's head off.

Prue, the redhead dancer from Chanel House, approached the table with a girl named Soofie, who was famous for inventing a new, nondamaging hair-straightening process she'd trademarked as Soofer Smooth. "We're so sorry about Renee," Prue said in a whisper, as if Renee had died. There had been a steady stream of girls stopping by to honor Renee's memory and pay their respects to the Jackie O's.

Triple shrugged, then stirred her Dancer's Detox tea. "She'll be fine. I heard *Dancing with the D-List* is coming back for another season."

Prue laughed with her shoulders.

"Either way." Soofer leaned a little closer to Charlie. "I'm sure whoever told on her had a perfectly good reason for it."

Allie's stomach sank on behalf of the ousted actress. Sure she'd miss her partner in crush-crime, but truth be told, they'd only known each other for a day. The bigger issue was what could have been. Or rather, what *should* have been. Wouldn't any normal girl with the power to vote someone off the island choose her ex's new picnic partner? Why was Allie still here?

Their aPods vibrated again. This time Allie knew better than to get her hopes up. Still, she did. And once again, another anonymous aJoke landed on her screen where Darwin's latest text should have been.

Q: Did you hear about Charlie's new clothing line?
A: It's called Spyware.

"Totally immature." Prue smiled at Charlie, clearly trying to get on her good side.

Charlie pushed her plate aside, obviously over more than breakfast, and Allie washed another bite of mushroom goo down with a sip of lemon spritzer, musing over how quickly life here had changed. Just yesterday, everyone had been fighting for the upper hand. Today it was for survival.

"Where are the boys?" Allie asked, after Prue finally left.

"Sydney said they're stuck eating with Shira," Skye reported.

"Since when is Sydney texting you?" Triple casually

ripped off a piece of her croissant. "I thought he liked Renee."

"It's a text, not a marriage proposal," Skye defended lightly.

Allie felt her fake eggs creep back up her throat. If Sydney had gotten over Renee in a matter of hours, what did that mean for her and Darwin? She wasn't sure she could handle another rejection—or another identity change. She knew her hair couldn't. Any more dye and it would break off at the roots.

Allie lifted her spoon, her reflection fun-housing in the convex silver base. She took comfort in seeing her beauty in the same way she imagined a singer would be happy to hear her own voice after a bout of laryngitis—glad her gift was still there even in times of crisis. But why wasn't it enough to compel Darwin to call her?

"Good morning, Becca Nash here from the Serena/ Venus House." A girl with slicked-back hair shook everyone's hand but Allie's, which managed to grab a fork just in time. Purell was scarce on Alpha Island. Better rude than ew-ed.

"I'm a journalism major, and let me just say, you haven't felt wind until you've tried to hold onto a microphone in that tornado simulator Shira built for us." She held her smile, then turned to Charlie. "Not that I'm complaining. I mean, I loved it. Blew the zits right off my face. And the experience was invaluable. I hope to get a lot of more it over the year." She smiled again. "A lot."

Charlie tried to return the smile. It looked more like she was holding in a burp.

"Mind if I ask you a few questions?"

The girls looked at each other in confusion.

"'It's better to know some of the questions than all of the answers,'" Thalia chimed in. "James Thurber."

"Shoot," Triple finally said, gathering her straight hair over one shoulder, then angling her body left.

"Great." Becca lifted a mascara wand–size video camera; the red record light was already on. Suddenly the girls appeared live on the Pavilion's oversize plasma.

Becca licked her bleached teeth and began. "Skye Hamilton, as a roommate of both the recently expelled Renee Foraday and Charlotte Deery—who has been indicted for espionage in the court of public opinion—what can you tell us?"

Everyone's attention was fixed on the broadcast, the scraps of their English muffins and energy smoothies forgotten on their tables. The Pavilion was utterly silent. Not a single utensil clinked.

Charlie lowered her head into her hands.

Skye smiled at the camera and cleared her throat. "No comment."

"So, do you think Charlie should remain at Alpha Academy?" Becca pressed.

"I'm not a spy, okay!" Charlie practically shouted.

Everyone gasped. Becca turned her mascara-camera toward her.

"*I* believe you." Skye gently touched her hand, then checked to make sure it was in the camera shot. "But can you prove it?"

Charlie balked. "What? How could I possibly—"

"I think it would really put people at ease and help clear your name if you could just—"

"Swear on Darwin's life," Allie interrupted. Charlie was neither gifted nor talented and had less drive than a Kia. The only alpha thing about her was her access to Shira Brazille. And Skye was so obviously afraid of being next, she was concealing Charlie's true identity like Cover Girl.

"That's stupid," Charlie hissed.

"Do it! Swear on Darwin's life that you're not Shira's spy and we'll believe you."

"I can't, that's crazy. We're not three years old." Charlie pushed back from the table with a screech and raced for the exit.

Skye arched one blond eyebrow directly at the camera lens.

"Well, I guess that answers that question," Triple put in.

With an outstretched arm, the reporter turned the camera on herself. "This is Becca Nash with a self-produced update. Because reporting is my passion and no news is no fun."

Finally free to react, the Pavilion erupted in a swirl of commentary.

Over the din, Thalia called, "Charlie, leaving before dismissal is against the rules." But Charlie kept running, forcing the muse to chase after her.

"Maybe she'll have to kick herself out," Triple joked, stretching her funny bone.

Allie nodded grimly and picked up her phone. If Charlie was the spy, then her time here was limited. She couldn't be sure why she hadn't been the first to go, but surely she would be the next. And she wasn't going to spend another night missing out on a once-in-a-lifetime opportunity. She positioned her thumbs over the aPod.

Allie J: I started a new song: No one kept Romeo and Juliet apart/Imagine if we changed the end and healed their heart? If you want to hear the rest, meet me tonight.

She pressed SEND and imagined the message sailing toward Darwin on the wings of an air kiss. Almost immediately, her aPod buzzed in her hands.

Darwin: Cant wait to hear it. C u l8r. ☺

And then it happened, her first shock of inspiration. The title of her memoir would be *Carpe Darwin: The story of a girl who risked it all for love*.

All she needed now was a happy ending.

18

Skye danced in the middle of the drum circle, her feet siphoning the beat from the all glass floor and distributing it to the rest of her body. Life pumped through her in a primal sort of way, transforming her from a skilled dancer into a wild creature of expression.

Triple, Prue, and the other tightly wound buns stretched on the sidelines.

"Skye, you can stop dancing," Mimi announced. "Good work."

Padding over to the barre, Skye squeezed in beside the other dancers and began loosening her joints.

"Any faster and you'd have traveled through time," Triple joked, lifting a leg to her ear like it was a cell phone.

The tight buns giggled.

"Any thinner and you'd *slip* though," Skye countered, not sure if what she said made sense. Not that she cared. She felt like a battery that had been recharged. All that moving around and physical freedom was just what she needed to shake the stress from the last few days. She felt clean. Clear. And ready to show Mimi what Westchester already knew.

That Skye was a star.

"Today we're going to learn how to do attitude turns," Mimi announced, the skirt on her bronze Lycra leo swinging with the same sultry swagger as her hips.

Skye scrunched her nose. Attitude turns were so second grade.

"I know you think you've had this turn mastered for years," Mimi said to Skye's nose. "But today I'm going to show you how to do it *properly*." She clapped twice. "Andrea and Sleeves, you're first."

No one moved.

"Andrea!" Mimi shouted at Triple.

"Oh," Triple smacked her bird chest in feigned horror. "Sorry, I'm so used to everyone calling me Tr—"

"And Sleeves," Mimi snapped her fingers at Skye. "Take center."

"Ready." Skye jazz-walked to the middle of the room, then rolled back her shoulders. Standing next to the model-dancer-actress felt like resting under a tree; Triple was tall, slender, and cast an enormous shadow. But could she give attitude?

"Music on," Mimi shouted.

The tribal drums resumed. It was an odd music choice for a standard jazz move, and Skye loved it. The less conventional the better.

"I want your best attitude turn. Move in a four-count even though the drums will be beating in an eight. This is all about control and grace. It's about tuning out your surroundings, feeling the choreography, and honoring its integrity."

Skye snuck a peek at Tweety and Ophelia. They looked just as confused as she felt. This was borderline insane. What was the point of dancing to the wrong beat? No one would ever ask her to do that in real—

"Five, six sev-uhn eight!" Mimi called. The drums beat a frenzied rendition of what sounded like the Ting Tings song "That's Not My Name."

Skye crossed her leg, plied in fourth like she was about to do a pirouette, and stopped. She felt like she was attempting that childish game of rubbing your belly and patting your head at the same time. The music was throwing her big-time.

"Sleeves, silence your mind and keep going," Mimi called.

Skye tried to shut out the raging music and focused on her four-count. *Cross one two three four . . . plié five six seven eight . . . clench butt two three four . . . lift leg . . .*

"Nice, Andrea, stay with it."

Suddenly, Skye lost count. Why did Mimi like Triple so much? The girl was a robot. Void of passion and—*oops* . . . Skye made the turn but landed too quickly. It reminded her of that time Robert Noble had tried to make out with her and kiss-missed. His lips had landed on her jaw and it had all been downhill from there.

"Music slow to four!" Mimi commanded. "Girls, give me attitude in double time."

Skye picked up the pace. She was starting to feel it now . . . *Cross leg . . . plié in fourth . . . clench butt . . . lift leg . . . and bring to attitude. Cross leg . . . plié in fourth . . . clench butt . . . lift leg . . . and bring to attitude.*

"Better, Sleeves," Mimi called. Her words were like defibrillators, sending electric jolts to Skye's heart.

Cross leg . . . plié in fourth . . . clench butt . . . lift leg . . . and bring to attitude.

"Nice energy!"

Cross legplié in fourth . . . clench buttlift leg . . . and bringtoattitude. . . . Cross legplié in fourth . . . clench buttlift leg . . . and bringtoattitude.

"A few more like that, Sleeves," Mimi urged.

Skye's heart was shocked into euphoria. Triple had gotten one shout-out. She'd gotten *three. Crosslegpliéinfourthclenchbuttliftlegandbringtoattitude.* She had hit her stride. *Crosslegpliéinfourthclenchbuttliftlegandbringtoattitude.* Mimi had finally noticed her talent. *Crosslegpliéinfourthclenchbuttliftlegandbringtoattitude.*

The thrill of it all made her turn faster and faster. *Crosslegplié-infourthclenchbuttliftlegandbringtoattitude*. Skye snuck a peek at Triple, who was a step and a half behind. Mimi was bound to make Skye her favorite now. Maybe she'd even back a line of dance sleeves named for her favorite student who— *Crosslegplié-infourthclenchbuttliftlegand* . . . Suddenly Skye's knee buckled.

"Ohmuhgud!"

Skye rolled over on her ankle, slammed into a glass wall like a bug on a windshield, and slid into darkness.

"Skye?"

Skye opened one turquoise eye. She was lying in a cloud of white, the scent of chamomile tea tickled her throbbing nose. "Is that where I am?" she mumbled. "In heaven?"

"It's me, Thalia," the muse said gently. "How is your ankle feeling?"

Skye peered at her ankle. It was mummified with layers of gauze and bandages the color of drugstore pantyhose. Was she hallucinating, or was it really bigger than her thigh? Tears sprang to her eyes.

"It hurts." She sniffled. Her mouth tasted like a sweaty leotard. "Why does it hurt so much?"

"'If you had not suffered as you have, there would be no depth to you, no humility, no compassion.'" Thalia smiled from the edge of her bed. "Eckhart Tolle said that."

"Is he dead too?"

"Just rest." Thalia removed the tea and gently covered Skye's elephant-ankle with the duvet. She tiptoed off, leaving Skye behind like she was a racehorse with a broken leg.

Skye replayed the fragmented memory of dance class again and again, trying to make sense of it all . . . and finally came to the only logical conclusion. She'd been dancing well, really well, and Triple had gotten jealous because she wasn't getting any Mimi-love and tripped her. That *had* to be it! It wasn't like Skye could have just fallen like some amateur.

"Okay, Skye. Ah-one-ah-two," she mumbled. Summoning all her strength, she lifted her shaky hands overhead and batted at her mom's ballet shoe like a kitten chasing a string, until it fell in her lap. With weak fingers, she began HAD No. 7: *Destroy Triple* . . .

But before she could finish, her ankle began to throb, her head swirled, and darkness claimed her once more.

The sun had set and something hard—a pen? A brush? The devil's pitchfork?—was poking Skye's spine. "Ow," she groaned. It sounded more like "Arughoi."

She rolled onto her side with the grace of an eighty-year-old and reached behind her back. Her headache pounded in protest as she gripped the hard satin . . . *Ohmuhgud!*

Skye shot straight up.

"Ahhhhhh," she moaned through the aftershocks of full-body pain, like a Hollywood heroine dislodging a knife from her own back. But this was far worse than a knife. It was the HADs shoe. And it was *empty!*

Littered around her bed were seven HADs, like crumpled scraps from fortune cookies. Her ankle felt like Savion Glover was tap-dancing all over it, and her eyes were having trouble focusing. Maybe this was just a dream. Or—

"Welcome to hell," Triple Threat growled.

—her biggest nightmare.

Allie J stood beside Triple, hands on her hips like a disappointed parent. A bouquet of shell-pink peonies hung from her palm.

"Hey," Skye managed with an exaggerated *take pity on me* grogginess. She pulled her swollen ankle out from under the down comforter for added effect.

"We came to check on you." Triple's light brown eyes bored into hers. She tapped her toe shoe and cleared her throat. "But I can see now that you don't need my help." She lifted the scrap of paper with *HAD No. 7: Destroy Triple* written on it. "In fact, I can see that you don't want me around at all."

"No." Skye tried to sit up. *Owie!* "It's not like that."

"Is it like this?" Allie J held up a napkin. *HAD No. 3: Crush Renee and Triple like chestnuts in a nutcracker.*

"You don't get it!" Skye insisted, her head whirling, her mouth dry.

"Oh, I get it," Allie J insisted. *"You're* the spy."

"Wait, what?" Suddenly the world snapped sharply into focus. "You think *I'm* the spy?" Skye screeched. *"Charlie's* the spy—you said so yourself!"

Triple waved the crumpled piece of paper like a victory flag. "Yeah, but she wasn't the one who wrote 'crush Renee' and made it come true." She sighed. "So I guess I'm next, huh? Can't take the competition, can you?"

Skye's hand closed around her mom's slipper, as if it could transport her to a fairy dance land where sugarplum fairies beat up girls named Triple Threat.

"That's a coincidence, not evidence." A note of urgency had crept into her voice, and hot, familiar pricks of tears knocked at the backs of her eyes, seeking escape. She tilted back her head, hoping to send them back to wherever it was tears came from.

"What does HAD even stand for? 'Heartless Alpha Desires'?" Triple asked, folding her arms over her chest. The starless sky had reduced her to a dark silhouette, but her rage was unmistakable.

"Hopes And Dreams," Skye muttered softly, as if sudden movement might trigger an avalanche of tears.

"You hope and dream of crushing your friends?" Allie J dropped the bouquet on the floor.

"Come on, A. J.," Skye pleaded, hoping a spontaneous nickname might endear the writer to her. "How could I rat you out to Shira when I'm just as guilty?"

Allie J considered this.

"Well, you obviously want *me* gone," Triple snapped.

"I may want you gone, but I'd never do anything about it," Skye blurted.

Allie J giggled.

Skye giggled too. "That came out wrong. I mean, these HADs are like a diary for me. That's all. I write down my thoughts and then get on with my life. I don't mean them."

"'Heartless Alpha *Diary*.'" Triple tossed her hair extensions over her shoulder self-righteously.

The fight drained out of Skye. She felt like the victim in the ballet *Giselle* who was forced to dance until she died. "I admit it, okay. I get jealous sometimes. I was the best dancer in my hometown and now I'm—"

"Not," Triple said flatly.

"I'm not the spy, okay? No one saw these HADs until now. I promise."

Triple and Allie J exchanged a *come on* glance. Frustration bubbled in Skye's veins like a Lush All That Jasmine Bath Bomb.

Allie J sighed. "I actually feel *bad* for Charlie."

"Totally." Triple shifted her feet into first. "I think it's time to send out an update."

Triple held her aPod in front of her, talking as she typed. "Beware of SPY Hamilton."

"Don't. Please," Skye begged. Her heart hurt more than her ankle. "It's not true!"

Ignoring her pleas, Triple and Allie J galloped down the glass staircase. For a moment, Skye sat in stunned silence.

Then Triple's head popped over the landing, a smile on her face. "One more thing."

Skye felt her spirits lift. Was Triple taking pity on her after all?

"It's a message from Mimi."

"Did she ask about me?"

"Yeah. She wanted to know how you ever got into this place." Triple cackled at her own crack and then hurried down the stairs.

Skye sank back into her pillows, feeling more deflated than a popped water bra. She wanted to dance away that conversation. Dance away her discovered HADs. Dance away her lack of friends. And most of all, dance away the disappointment that was sure to wrinkle her mother's Botoxed face when she got sent home.

But dancing was no longer an option.

19

Charlie squeezed the tiny flash drive in her hand as she read the news ticker that slithered across the windows outside Shira's office.

Skye Hamilton is recovering from a fall in Mimi's dance class. She will live but will she live it down? . . . LoChang is picking up a third major. In addition to engineering and sculpting she has added string instruments . . . Animal plastic surgery phenom Kutya Slavin gave a beautiful nose job and tummy tuck to Poncho the Chihuahua. The results are inspiring. . . .

It was hard to focus on the *Island Update* when the key to her future lay in her sweaty palm. It had taken all night and most of the day, but it was finally time to show Shira what she could contribute—or rather, how she *had* contributed to building the Brazillionaire's precious academy. So what if her mum always said bragging was tacky? Charlie was just as qualified as the girls who'd actually applied. And her application, essay, design blueprints, tech specs, and international education would prove it beyond a shadow of a doubt.

Fiona set a white mug on the ice-block table. A stream of coffee rained down from above.

"No thanks." Charlie smiled graciously at the assistant. But no sleep, no food, and the rumbling churn of anxiety had left her wired enough.

"Try it," Fiona urged, her mud brown eyes unwavering. "Trust me."

Leaning forward in her chair, Charlie politely lifted the cup to her mouth. It smelled like Bee. "You got the recipe." She sipped.

"Miracles do happen, you know." Fiona grinned, sounding more like a nun than a beaten-down rebound assistant.

"I guess." Charlie sighed, remembering that her mom had sent Shira the recipe as a thank-you.

A green light above Shira's door illuminated.

"She'll see you now," Fiona said.

"Thanks." Charlie placed the empty cup back on the table, then pressed her sweaty hands into the ice. The chilly burn cooled her nerves.

"Good luck." Fiona waved.

Like Dorothy approaching the Wizard, Charlie crept with caution toward the alpha's open door.

"Beyoncé, it's not that we don't appreciate the offer, luv,

it's just that I'm not taking any guest lecturers from the mainland at this time. Island policy, lolly. Nothing personal." Shira waved for Charlie to come in and sit down while she wrapped up her call. As always, she wore round black glasses, a matching maxidress, and an air of superiority.

Behind her Lucite, Australia-shaped desk, five new portraits of her sons were displayed on the floating shelf. Darwin's brown locks were standing up like he'd just run his fingers through them. She stared at his face, his freckle, and his hazel eyes without inhibition, like he was art hung for her to admire. There were no traces of guilt, longing, or pain anywhere inside her. Just appreciation. For the first time in days, just appreciation. He was perfect.

Suddenly Darwin blinked, and Charlie gasped. She waved just in case the live feed went both ways, but Darwin didn't respond.

"I know, and I appreciate your enthusiasm," Shira said into her Bluetooth, sounding bored.

Next to Darwin's frame, Dingo was slouched over a notebook, undoubtedly planning his next elaborate prank. Taz was swinging from a ceiling fan. Sydney was drying his eyes on the sleeve of his blazer. And Melbourne was completely still, probably working on his mannequin-modeling poses.

"You are at the top of my list should the ban on outside influences ever lift, okay? Love to Jay. G'day." Shira pressed a recessed button on her Lucite desk and the call was done.

"Celebrities. They're more beastly than Komodo dragons." Shira swiveled toward her guest. "Tim Tam?" She gestured to the tray of imported Australian cookies.

Charlie popped one in her mouth and luxuriated in their melty chocolate goodness. Shira took a cookie as well, and they chewed in comfortable silence. For a second, Charlie forgot all about their recent drama—or trauma, rather—and basked in the joy of sharing a delicious snack with a woman she'd known her entire life. It was nice to just sit and—*wait a minute!* Charlie swallowed hard, then pushed the plate aside. This wasn't companionship. It was Stockholm syndrome; a condition where kidnapping victims BFFed their captors. It seemed highly improbable that Charlie could find pleasure in the presence of this particular tormentor. But in her vulnerable state—no friends, no boyfriend, no mother, no sleep, Tim Tams—she did. And so she reminded herself that Shira's small kindness wasn't kindness at all—just an extravagance to reinforce good behavior.

Charlie smacked the flash drive down on Shira's desk.

"What's this?" Shira looked but didn't touch.

"My Alpha Academy application. The essay, the transcripts—everything I would have needed to get in on my own," she said, the assertive words harder to pass than a kidney stone. "I hope you'll see that I belong here and lift the conditions placed on my admission—namely the breakup with Darwin and the forced resignation of Bee Deery."

Charlie sat still, listening for the crack of thunder Shira

was sure to rain down on her. But all she heard was her heart beating in her ears.

Shira tapped her long fingernails on the Lucite desk and then pushed the drive back to Charlie. "*Rejected.*"

"You're not even going to look at it?" Charlie asked, stunned. She'd assumed Shira would at least be curious.

"I don't have to. I've known you for fourteen years, lolly."

"Then you should know I don't want to be your spy."

Shira calmly pushed her dark glasses up the bridge of her sharp nose. "Oh, my darling girl. Spy? That sounds so Disney. Allow me to suggest a more sophisticated moniker. Perhaps ABS: Alpha Behavior Surveillance."

Charlie thought about the last time she'd made eggs for Darwin. They had been left alone in a villa in Tuscany with a fridge full of nothing but eggs and condiments. She'd burned the omelets to a sad, plasticky lump. She'd quickly covered them in ketchup and renamed the dish Eggs Marinara. No matter what it was called, it had still left a bad taste in her mouth.

"I can't do it."

Shira folded her arms across her chest and leaned backward. "If you're half as smart as you claim, you should understand the unique benefits of this offer."

Charlie's eyebrow lift signaled that she had no clue what Shira was taking about.

"You're in the unique position of being the only girl all but guaranteed to make it to the final two."

"That's a benefit? To be your spy until the real alpha is revealed?"

"ABS."

"Fine, whatever you want to call it. But what's the point of sticking around if I don't even have a fair chance?" Charlie laughed bitterly as she realized there was no scenario—not now or ever—in which Shira would see Charlie as a true contender. She hated herself for ever having believed otherwise.

"Number two is still something to be proud of"—Shira lowered her voice—"for most people." She looked over at the doorway, where Fiona hovered, just like Bee used to.

Shira pushed back from the desk and stood, smoothing down her flowing black dress. "Excuse me—I have to approve the new font for the *Island Updates*," she said, following Fiona out the door. "The old one was so . . . *common*, don'tcha think?" She winked at Charlie, then slipped out.

Charlie squeezed her hands into angry red fists. She hated Shira more than the stomach flu. More than girls who called her Charlie Brown-nose. Even more than . . .

Charlie blinked. Dingo's image was moving. He was slinking across his bedroom toward the life-sized portrait of his father. After a couple of beeps, the picture swung open and Dingo disappeared inside.

"Oh my God." Charlie sat ramrod straight in her chair.

Like a match igniting off a lit candle, her brain cells sparked a brilliant idea.

In the final week before school opened, she had invented one last gem for her mother. With so many buildings and tunnels and so much technology to account for, Bee and Shira would have had to keep over a hundred keys with them at all times. So Charlie had created a gold skeleton key that overrode every security system on the island. Shira had had it in her hands just the other day . . .

If she could get it somehow and give it to the Jackie O's, they could meet the boys in the tunnels, undetected. And they'd know that Charlie was on their side, even if she was the ABS. They'd be trusted friends in no time. Sisters in arms. The only flaw, aside from a life in prison should she get caught, was that she'd be helping Allie J and Darwin fall in love.

The bitter taste of half-digested Tim Tams coated her throat. That was the last thing she needed. But if she wanted to stay at the academy, she had to be an ABS. And she wanted to stay. Seeing Darwin with someone else was better than not seeing him at all.

Charlie sighed and looked around the office. Last time, the gold device had been on Shira's desk. But not today. All she saw was the bookshelf, the picture frames, the black-and-white globe, the giant book about Shira's life, the— wait, backtrack . . . *the black-and-white globe!*

If she'd learned *anything* from her time with Darwin, it was where Shira hid her keys.

Without another thought, she flicked the "pin" that unlocked the globe (Shira's hometown of Adelaide, where she'd met her late husband). Sure enough, there was the spare key, blinking like a puppy at a pet store, begging her to take it home.

Quickly, she slid it into her skirt pocket and closed the globe just as the office door swung back open. She spun around, heart pounding.

"Font approved. Now, where were we?"

"I was just going," Charlie blurted, inching toward the door.

"Not so fast." Shira's crispness stopped her short.

Charlie slowly turned on the heels of her clear gladiators, her pulse racing. "Yes?" She willed her voice not to shake.

"Do we have an agreement?" Shira blinked innocently.

"Oh yeah." Charlie smiled in true relief. "I thought about it and you were right. ABS is a good offer for a girl like me." She backed into the glass atrium hallway and forced herself to walk away slowly.

But the second she got outside, she broke into a run.

The night air smelled of orange citrus blossoms and hope. If Bee could have seen her now, she'd have marched Charlie back in and made her return the key. But Charlie didn't care. Shira had taken so much from her; it was only fair she take something from Shira. And all she asked for in return were some friends.

And revenge.

20

Allie J: D, I'm here

Allie J: R u hiding?

Allie J: Super dark. Getting cold.

Allie J: Um, did u hear that? Are there wolves on the island?

Allie J: Heading back before I'm attacked.

Allie J: Hope they didn't get you.

Allie J: Bye.

21

Allie followed the APS on her aPod toward the undisclosed location of today's writing class. Despite the chirping birds and radiant sunshine, she felt like the walking dead, en route to her own funeral.

Texting alone in the dark the night before, surrounded by nocturnal beasts, while waiting for a boy crush who never showed had been more painful than a full-facial threading. Had Charlie stolen him back? Had he found someone new? Was he pulling away after the mortifying triangle poem incident? Maybe he'd discovered Trina's art and was heading for the mainland to propose. Not that it mattered. The damage had been done. Allie's heart was more tattered than the bottoms of her feet, her confidence reduced to the size of her kohl-mole.

"Keep west. The Eros Sculpture Garden will appear in approximately ninety-seven paces . . ." the British voice from her aPod instructed. "Five steps until you hit the beach . . ."

201

Her aching bare feet sighed with relief as they sank into the pink sand–covered path that led to the Eros Garden. Palm trees surrounded the walkway, and a soft breeze that smelled like coffee rustled Allie's black hair.

"Allie J!" someone breathed on the back of her neck.

"Ahh!" Allie gasped. She turned to find Hannah standing behind her.

"Finally," Hannah panted. "I've been calling your name. Who were you talking to?"

Allie felt her cheeks redden. During times of extreme stress she sometimes talked to herself.

"Notice anything different?" Hannah struck a pose. It was more scarecrow than supermodel, and Allie had to laugh.

She tapped a Purell-thirsty finger against her lips. "Your skin doesn't look as corpse-ish, your hair isn't so witchy black, and you're not spackled in goth makeup." The only thing that looked the same was the sapphire stud that sparkled in Hannah's left nostril. And with all of the changes, it looked borderline cool.

"Well, Keifer's all about being real," Hannah explained, continuing down the path. "Sooooo, why not go natural? You know, to honor the true essence of writing. And of course, the true essence of me."

Envy stung Allie like a blast of deodorant on freshly shaved pits. If only she could strip away her disguise and honor *her* true essence. But what exactly was that? A talent-less mall model with a knack for getting her heart broken? These days, she felt about as natural as a little blue packet of Equal.

Allie's aPod blinged like she'd hit the jackpot. "Welcome to Eros Sculpture Garden!" the Brit said primly.

Tongue-shaped pools of water licked the shore, which was made of pink sand and studded with a dozen famous lovers carved in stone: Adam and Eve, Romeo and Juliet, Tristan and Isolde, Cupid and Psyche, Krishna and Radha, Patrick Dempsey and his unfamous wife. The other students trickled onto the beach. Circling the statues, they reached out delicately and poked them with trepidation, like they just might come to life.

Seeing these lovers, side by side for all eternity, meant at least six relationships had stood the test of time. There was a time when Allie thought she'd be number seven. Not anymore.

White-winged doves drifted overhead. They cooed love haikus while butterfly couples rested on the rocky shoulders of timeless lovers, basking in the warmth of their union. Palm fronds tangled briefly every time a breeze blew, like secret sweethearts desperate to touch when no one's looking.

Serious-leh? Was there anything more depressing than standing in a love garden with a twice-baked broken heart and a pretentious she-writer with coffee breath?

Um, no.

"Why would Shira create a love garden when she's so against boys?" Allie asked, to avoid crying.

"You know what they say." Hannah leaned closer. "Those who can't do, teach."

"Look!" Allie point-shouted, escaping Hannah's java breath before her contacts fogged. Then she scampered toward the most alluring statue of all. Hunched over the water, it gazed at its own reflection with extreme intensity. Like her, he had the unfortunate fate of being single in a garden of love.

As she searched for an explanation plaque or anything that might explain his sorry relationship status, a hint of jasmine signaled that she was no longer alone.

"Captivating, isn't it?" Keifer rubbed the statue's back affectionately. Her choppy black bangs were pinned to the side of her face, allowing her deep red lipstick to take center stage.

"Narcissus was so vain that he fell in love with his own reflection and drowned." She leveled her eyes at Allie. "What do you think about that?"

Uh, I know how the drowning part feels, she wanted to say. But instead she reached deep into her soul and said, "His parents must have been so upset."

"I think it's a metaphor for people who use love as a mirror. Instead of seeing the other person, they see themselves.

Always themselves. And how that person reflects on them. Sad, isn't it?" With that, Keifer turned on her heel and walked away without another word.

Confusing was more like it. Was Keifer trying to tell her something? It wasn't like Allie was in love with herself. She *hated* her black hair. Besides, she was very much in like with Darwin. And in heartbreak with Fletcher. Plus she happened to be an excellent swimmer.

Just then Darwin appeared on the beach and the world went slo-mo. His caramel-colored waves fluttered around his head, each perfect strand glinting in the sunlight.

He strolled over to the Adam and Eve statues. His long, easy strides were effortless compared to Fletch's well-rehearsed strut. With each step, sand billowed around him, as if every granule was jumping up to kiss his tanned legs. Charlie glanced up at him and smiled awkwardly. Darwin lowered his head but remained by the statues—and Charlie. Barefoot, their toes looked happy to see each other. Their mouths did not.

Allie felt like she was watching a chick flick on mute— the kind that left her in a mess of tears before the first act had even ended.

Keifer whistled shrilly, and everyone gathered around. Dry sand caked Allie's wet feet and took shelter between her toes. Sand that other barefoot people had stood in. *Ew!* If she ever got Reneed, surgical foot scraping would be at the top of her to-do list.

"Join hands," Keifer said, offering her palms to Bridgette and Tatiana.

Allie was stuck between Hannah and Yara; an a-hole and a C-cup. Thankfully, she had a little bit of Purell on standby.

Charlie turned a Kermity shade of green and reached for Darwin's hand. He took it with a mix of longing and disgust, like a hungry vegetarian waiter serving a burger.

How was this happening again? Weren't beautiful people supposed to be in the *center* of love triangles—not impaled by their sharp points?

"Everyone please close your eyes," Keifer whispered.

Everyone did but Allie. Through her green lenses, she peered across the circle at Darwin. His expression was tight and strained, like he was holding in a poo. The possibility that he might not be enjoying Charlie's hand warmed Allie's icy insides. But not enough to melt them. He'd have to look her in the eye for that to happen.

"A good writer describes the world without platitudes..." Keifer began her morning lecture.

Allie searched her classmates through the blur of a scrunched eye. Was she the only who had no idea what *platitudes* meant?

"And a *great* writer describes it with emotions." Keifer paused, allowing her words to penetrate her pupils' champagne-colored blouses and fill their hearts with hope.

"Today's in-class assignment is to write about the euphoria of love as inspired by this garden. Grab your tablets, find a spot in the sand by your favorite statue, and begin." Keifer picked up some sand and let it slip through her fingers as through an hourglass. "You have ten minutes."

Everyone opened their eyes and raced to get started.

Allie quickly squeezed a squirt of Purell and rubbed vigorously. But for the first time ever, her hands didn't want to sanitize—they wanted to write. She leaned against Narcissus's quads and tried to ignore the fact that Darwin was ignoring her. Then she let herself go.

Only once did she let her eyeballs wander—Darwin had an adorable snarl on his lips and he tapped his tablet with purpose. Hannah twirled her nose ring thoughtfully. And the tip of Charlie's tongue poked out of her mouth as she searched the cloudless sky for the perfect word.

"Time," Keifer called, her fingers drained of sand.

Allie put down her tablet, feeling lighter—like the first time she'd shaved her legs.

She gazed out at the water, wondering if maybe Narcissus had had the right idea, falling in love with himself. She would never dump herself for Charlie. Or Trina.

"Allie J, this should be perfect for you," Keifer's voice cut through her daydream. "Your songs always end on a positive note. Why don't you start us off today?"

The sun beat down on the back of her neck, but it was

the seven sets of eyes on her that made her sweat. Darwin's hazel irises bored into hers, and she couldn't help but feel like he was urging her to steer clear of triangles.

Casting her own eyes down at her screen, she blocked everything, and everyone, out. She could do this. . . .

"Everything here is bright and cheery like a Crest Whit-estrip laugh. You could snap a shot with your eyes closed and still score a postcard-perfect picture. Every inch of sand and every sculpted smile is here to make me feel my heart. And I do. But like theirs, mine has turned to stone."

Allie looked up and grinned. She was ready to accept her "most improved" award.

Yara was biting her bottom lip so hard it had turned white. A plastic surgeon couldn't have raised Hannah's brows any higher. Charlie was staring at the sand, Darwin at the ocean.

Keifer cleared her throat. "Can you explain your piece to us? Where were you?"

Every time Keifer asked a question, Allie felt like she was under the bright lights of an interrogator. Back home, she and her teachers had a *don't ask, don't answer* relationship. Now, even her teeth were nervous. "I was . . . I *was* right here."

A few of the girls giggled.

Keifer shook her head in obvious disappointment. "Allie J, I asked you to write about euphoric love and you gave me despair."

Allie pretzeled her arms across her chest defensively. "You said to reach inside, and that's what I found."

Weren't her stories supposed to be objective? Or was it subjective? Whatever. Wasn't she allowed to write what she wanted?

"Allie J, my assignments are not *suggestions*." Keifer tucked a strand of black hair behind her earringless ear. "I asked for a description of a warm, loving place and you drained it of life and turned it to rock."

Are you kidding me? Allie wanted to scream. She'd once rolled down a runway in the Riverside Mall in a bikini and skates, but Keifer was the one who made her feel naked. *But I'm trying! I'm finally trying!* A tidal wave of anxiety crashed over her, and Allie couldn't bear it any more. Throwing her tablet in the sand, she stood up and ran.

"Allie J!" Keifer called. "Stop!"

But Allie couldn't. She bolted as fast as her bare feet would take her, as if she were trying to outrun herself, trying to shed her flawless skin and the expectations that came with it.

She reached the tree line and returned to the woods without looking back.

"Allie J!" Keifer tried again.

But Allie J wasn't her name, and she wasn't answering to it. Not anymore.

22

THEATER OF DIONYSUS
HONE IT: FOR DANCERS
WEDNESDAY, SEPTEMBER 8TH
2:44 P.M.

Skye sat in the corner of the dance studio elevating her swollen ankle on a Recovery Lounger. The gel-filled La-Z-Boy alternated from hot to cold every twenty minutes to keep injuries from turning into surgeries. It also worked wonders on swelling heads. One more class on the sidelines and Skye's ego would be the size of an airbrushed pore.

Mimi sashayed by while demonstrating a cabriole. She landed a yard away from Skye's foot and gasped, "Music, pause!" Every dancer stopped along with the music, and Mimi heel-toed over to the Recovery Lounger. She gripped her hips. "Sleeves, have you completely given up?"

"Of course not, no." Skye's melting spine stiffened.

What was Mimi talking about? She had spent the better part of an hour committing every step to memory; couldn't she see Skye's eyes working overtime? Her mind's feet were moving to Mimi's choreography, her ankle throbbing to the beat of the smoky jazz. Dutifully, she watched the girls embody trees, while she left like a felled sequoia gathering moss.

"What is that?" Mimi asked Skye's dance shoe. The gold satin was marred with crust that looked like toothpaste.

Triple smirked, as if wanting the class to know she was partly responsible.

"I don't know," Skye lied. But come on, what was she supposed to say? My *housemates wrote* Spy Hamilton *in shaving cream and I stepped in it on my way to the bathroom? It's a case of mistaken spydentity? Please don't send me home?*

Mimi shook her head. "A true dancer always knows what's on her shoes." With that, she strutted back to the front of the class, mindful of where her insured feet were walking.

The others turned their backs to Skye as though her swollen ankle was more contagious than swine flu. Even Tweety and Ophelia seemed disinterested in a *you're only as good as your last soutenu* sort of way. And they were kind of right. What good was a girl with no friends and no game? Unless they planned on sacrificing her to the alpha gods or donating her organs to the science majors, Skye would be boarding a PAP by sundown.

Mimi clapped sharply. "Even the tiniest flaws can sabotage your performance. And most of these flaws are bad habits you picked up when you were just starting out." A black corkscrew curl escaped her bun and bounced alongside her cheek. Skye envied its playful giddiness and natural shine, two qualities she no longer possessed.

Mimi grabbed her aPod off the holster around her hips and pressed some buttons. Six holograms flickered to life.

"Wow!"

"Amazing!"

"Is that me?"

"Ohmuhgud!"

Staring at Skye from the other end of the Recovery Lounger was a little girl dressed in a tutu. Her wavy blond hair had been French-braided to bathing-cap tightness. Her broad smile was missing two teeth, and white-blond brows sat like silky bows on top of Tiffany box blue eyes.

"Girls, meet your younger selves." Mimi announced with the crazed smile of a mad scientist. Her brown, almond-shaped eyes radiated pride. "We created a computer composite based on the recital tapes you sent with your applications. I have pinpointed the exact moment you strayed from perfection and would like you to discover it as well. We must locate and understand the problem before we can fix it."

Triple raised her hand and spoke. "Um, excuse me, Mimi, but um, what if we don't have a problem?"

"Yeah," echoed some of the others.

The teacher's ribs lunged up against her bronze bodysuit, then pulled back, like an angry attack dog chained to a fence. "Oh, you have flaws, Andrea, believe me. Starting with your need to give yourself a nickname so everyone knows you have talent. But that's an issue for the psych department.

I'm here to focus on your physical flaws, of which you have several. You all do."

Skye rolled her wrists nervously, willing Mimi to avoid rattling them off in public.

"For example"—Mimi paced the row of five—"Andrea, you're precise, but you lack passion. I watch you dance and I think back to the time I practiced kissing on my mirror. I hit my mark but felt nothing."

Tweety twittered.

"I don't know what you're laughing about, Lacey." Mimi circled the bobbleheaded girl. "You're built like a lollipop. If you want to stop sucking, put more power below the neck, or your skull will always upstage you."

The temperature on the Recovery Lounger switched to icy. But Skye couldn't stop sweating as Mimi made her rounds.

"Sadie, save the chopping for your culinary classes. In here I want smooth transitions. Ophelia, I'm going to hack off that braid if you don't bun it up. It's throwing off your balance. We dance with our hearts, not our hair. Prue, you're tight."

Prue beamed relief.

"Eat nothing but bran for three days straight. If that doesn't loosen your blockage, consider a career as a mannequin. And Sleeves . . ." Mimi paused to tuck the errant curl back into submission. "Stop searching for love in the studio. Find it within yourself. If you don't, you'll bump up against walls for the rest of your life. Your freestyle isn't dazzling—it's distracting. Perfect the moves, then add the grooves."

The girls stood in silent horror. After a lifetime of being told they were the best of the best, they had been reduced to puddles of sweat—Skye included. Only her sweat had been frozen into a sheet of salty ice, thanks to the Recovery Lounger.

Was Mimi right about her? Maybe. After all, she was right about the others. But as Skye replayed the teacher's words, she felt her cryogenically frozen spirits lift. Mimi's critique was about her personality, not her poise. Maybe she had to strip away all of that confidence and open her mind. Listen to her teachers and rebuild her foundation. Kind of like Icarus putting a new coat of wax on his melted wings and vowing not to fly so high next time. Sure, Icarus was dead, but Skye was just broken. There was still time. She still had a chance.

"I want you to spend the remainder of the class studying your younger selves to see if you can tap into the moment your skills soured." Mimi clapped. "Music on. Dancers, begin."

The girls watched in wonder as their mini me's danced across the studio, showcasing routines they hadn't seen in years.

Skye's mini took a seat on the arm of the Recovery Lounger, indifferent to the cold.

"Dance," Skye commanded, feeling semi-insane talking to the ghost of Skye past.

The girl glanced at Mimi, then the other dancers, and shook her head no.

"Why not?" Skye pressed.

"No one is watching. I'll wait until they're paying attention to me. Then I'll dance."

Problem identified.

Skye had spent her life dancing for others: Natasha, Madame P, her friends, her crushes . . .

Did she love dancing or performing? It was a hard question to answer. No one had ever made her think about it until now. She remembered a time when dance was the only thing that mattered. It was before she was good enough to be noticed. Before she got addicted to applause. Before it became the thing that made her special.

"Sorry," Skye heard herself apologizing to the flickering girl.

"For what?"

"For everything," Skye mumbled, thinking of how she'd thought spa-ing with girls who weren't even talking to her now had seemed more important than practicing. How flirting with Taz could have gotten her expelled. How trying to out-dance Triple had landed her in chair that went hot and cold more times than Blair and Nate.

Pushing her butt off the lounger, Skye grinned at her younger self. "Who cares who's looking. Let's dance! I'll watch you."

Little Skye yipped with excitement and broke into the jazz sequence from her first recital at age five.

Skye tested her ankle on a simple barrel turn. *Owie!* Agony reverberated through her body like one of those forked prongs used to test musical pitch. On the pain scale— one being a paper cut and ten being a wood chipper—it was a six.

She tried again. "Ophf!" The move cranked her pain to a nine and she fell to her knees. Thankfully, Mimi was too busy patting Triple on the back to notice.

"Music off!" Mimi called, and Skye crawled back to the lounger. A new, deep shade of plum mottled her screaming ankle.

"Time to say goodbye to your pasts," Mimi announced. "Forever."

A chorus of "bye"s echoed around the glass studio. Skye wrapped her arms around her younger self until she was holding nothing but air.

"You are no longer Shira's handpicked six-pack of wun- derkind dancers. You are mindless slabs of clay waiting to be shaped by my hands, and my hands only." Mimi glared at Skye when she said *slab.* "Tonight I want you to work on exorcising your demons. Dance today's routine until your flaws slough off like old skin and then wash them down the drain. I will grade you on your progress tomorrow." She swung her quilted black dancer bag over her shoulder and glided out without another word.

Prue grimaced as she eased her feet out of her shoes.

Her toes were bleeding. Ophelia shook her hair out. Tweety massaged her neck. And Mercedes dropped to the floor like a starfish.

"Come on! We've got work to do." Triple moved for her bag, nodding for the other girls to join her. But they took a collective pause, not quite ready to rejoin the star who'd so outshined them yet again.

"I can't move," Prue whined.

"What's the point?" Ophelia asked. "I can't change ten years of dancing habits overnight."

"I think I'm going to focus on culinary and drop dance down to a hobby." The redhead sighed.

Skye clapped the girls to attention. "Don't give up, Mercedes!"

"It's Sadie," the redhead corrected.

"Oops."

"Look who's talking." Prue rubbed her toes. "You gave up days ago."

"How is getting injured giving up?" Skye snapped, shifting to her strong ankle. "I may have been sitting on the sidelines, but I've been watching. And I know this routine better than any of you. I also happen to agree with Mimi. We can all stand improving. And since I can't do, I'll coach," Skye blurted. "If anyone is interested."

"What's in it for you?" Sadie sat up and reached for her toes. "Bragging rights?"

"I won't even mention it to Mimi. I just want to get back to dancing. And this is the only way I can . . . for now." She slipped on her black lace sleeves, feeling like Superman after a way-too-long stint as Clark Kent.

Skye's heart beat wildly while they considered her impulsive proposal.

"I wonder what Mimi would say about you molding her slabs." Triple leaned against the barre, an amused expression on her face.

"Where I come from, professionals don't care where good ideas come from, as long as they come. And Sadie, who knows? Maybe the Robot is making a comeback. But I doubt it." With that, Skye limped for the door, taking her sweet time.

"Skye, wait!" Ophelia called. "Can you meet us here after dinner?"

"I was already planning on it." Skye smiled to herself and kept on limping.

Coaching was hardly her passion. Back home she'd done it to improve the BADS brand and help her BFFs. These girls weren't exactly her besties, but maybe that was the point. She'd be doing it strictly out of love for the craft— not for the claps that came with. It would be her opportunity to teach Little Skye the true meaning of dedication—and maybe even make a few friends for Big Skye in the process.

23

"RE-JEC-TED!"

"Darn it!" Charlie frustration-smacked the coin-tiled shower wall. "Owie, owie, owie!" She pressed her lips against her throbbing hand, urging both into silence.

Her aPod kept beeping, signaling that she was supposed to be in the DAM (Dominating Alpha Males) seminar, but instead she was hiding out in a stall decorated in international currency, cowering from seven showerheads spraying lavender-infused water.

Due to the expectation of privacy that comes with being in a bathroom, Shira couldn't install cameras here without breaking the law. So in spite of the billowing steam and hair-curling humidity, it was the perfect location to crack the combination of the skeleton key.

Unfortunately, the only things opening so far were her pores.

219

"Okay, Shira. Let's try your zip code." Charlie punched in "6-6-6" with a sly giggle.

"RE-JEC-TED!" the robotic key-voice answered back.

A drop of water landed on her cheek like a hot tear. She brushed it away impatiently.

She tried the founding date of AlphaGirl International: 9-1-9-1-9-9-0.

"RE-JEC-TED!"

3-5. Shira's press age.

4-3. Her real age.

"RE-JEC-TED! RE-JEC-TED!"

4-2. Darwin's birthday.

5-2-4. Melbourne's birthday.

9-1-9. Sydney's birthday.

8-9. Taz and Dingo's birthdays.

2-2-6-3-9. Bandy, Shira's late husband's name, spelled out on the keypad.

3-5-8-3-3-9. Fluffy, the name of her childhood chinchilla.

5-4-5-5-3-7. Killer, the name of her recently deceased cat.

7-2-8-2-6. Satan, Shira's father. Kidding!

2-5-7-4-2. Alpha.

1-7-8-3. The number of offices Shira had worldwide.

6-7-9-1. The number of assistants Shira had hired.

6-7-9-0. The number of assistants Shira had fired. (Technically, Bee had quit.)

1. Shira's favorite number.

9-5. The day Shira succeeded in breaking up Charlie and Darwin.

"RE-JEC-TED! RE-JEC-TED! RE-JEC-TED! RE-JEC-TED! RE-JEC-TED! RE-JEC-TED! RE-JEC-TED! RE-JEC-TED! RE-JEC-TED! RE-JEC-TED! RE-JEC-TED! RE-JEC-TED!"

"ARGGGG!" Charlie banged her head against some pesos. Even a key was rejecting her. Steam, frustration, and anxiety were making it hard to breathe.

Think, Charlie. THINK!

There was no way Shira had picked something random. A woman who controlled the weather would not leave anything to chance.

Charlie twirled her cameo bracelets around her wrist. She twisted so hard that one of the cameos flew open, and her mom's picture smiled up at her.

Of course!

No wonder she couldn't crack the Brazille Code—Shira hadn't created it. Bee had. Bee planned everything for Shira—why not this?

And Charlie knew without hesitation what was important to her mother.

2-4-2-7-5-4-3. Charlie.

"AC-SESS GRANT-ED."

"Ha!" Charlie laughed, kicking the spray of water with her feet. "I did it!"

In just a few short hours she'd introduce the Jackie O's to the tunnels, where Dingo had disappeared to when he'd slipped behind Bandy's portrait. It was the only place other than the bathrooms where Shira's digital army couldn't find them. But in addition to making friends, she'd be delivering Allie J to Darwin. Suddenly Charlie's palms started sweating and she found it hard to breathe. It was kind of like setting up a playdate between a coyote and your new puppy. But she'd broken Darwin's heart, and the least she could do was help mend it. And if all went according to plan, she'd have a house full of new BFFs mending hers.

Now all Charlie had to do was stay dry and wait. . . .

Finally the bathroom door opened. Bare feet slapped against the heated marble.

"Allie J? C'mere," Charlie whispered from the shower. "Bring shaving cream."

"Ew, no way!"

Charlie giggled to herself, thinking of how that must have sounded.

"Trust me, it's not creepy, I swear."

"Why should I believe you?" Allie J whisper-shouted.

Charlie pressed her mouth against the slight crack in the stall door. "Because I have something for you."

"Double ew!" Allie J sounded repulsed. "I like boys, okay?"

Charlie rolled her eyes. "I know. That's what I have for you."

Allie J paused. "Huh?"

Charlie inhaled deeply, bracing herself, or rather forcing herself, to say the next word.

"What are you talking about?" Allie snapped.

"Darwin." Charlie swallowed back the bitter taste of sacrifice. Her head took a dizzying dip. It was out there. There was no turning back.

Allie J opened the stall with trepidation, can of Pure Silk in hand. "If this is some ploy to get me to help you shave some hard-to-reach area, I'm so not—"

Charlie rolled her eyes and pulled Allie J into the shower.

"Ahhhhhh!" Water sprayed all over her. "My hair!"

She panic-stuffed her black hair into the back of her champagne-colored blouse in a very not-so-down-to-earth sort of way; odd behavior for someone who cruised communal bathrooms barefoot.

"Shhhhh!" Charlie grabbed the can of shaving cream and wrote *I SPY* on her right leg, in case Thalia's superhuman ears were in range. The admission smelled like baby oil and relief.

"I knew it!" Allie J exclaimed, still panic-stuffing. "Wait. Why are you telling me?"

DBL AGENT Charlie spelled out on her left thigh, then put the can down.

"Why are you—"

Charlie covered Allie J's mouth.

Allie J grabbed the can and wrote in the spaces between the straps on her gladiators.

Y R U TELLING ME?

WANT FRIENDS, Charlie sprayed onto her arm. She hated how pathetic that sounded but decided not to care. It was the truth.

"Why would I trust you?" Allie J asked aloud.

Charlie lifted the gold key, then wrote: *STOLE FROM S. OPENS TUNNELS SO WE CAN MEET BOYS.*

Allie J's green eyes blinked in genuine surprise. Then they hardened into emerald stones. "Oh, I get it. You're setting me up so I get sent home and you can have Darwin all to yourself."

Charlie shook her head. For a moment she couldn't believe that she was really trying to force the love of her life on a super-eligible bachelorette. "He doesn't want me anymore," she managed. "He likes you."

Allie J squinted like she was trying to spot Charlie in the distance.

"'Boys come and go, but in the end I see, it's my friends

224

who complete me . . .'" she said, quoting the chorus of "I Like My Boys Like Salad Dressing—On the Side."

"Huh?" Allie J blinked in confusion.

"Do you even believe your own lyrics?" A spray of water found its way into Charlie's mouth. She spit it out.

A look of panic crossed Allie J's pretty face. "No I-I do," she stammered. "Of course I do."

"Then you understand what I'm talking about. Darwin was my whole life. And now that we're done, I have nothing. I want to move on. I want friends."

"Fine," Allie J. said. "But we should include Skye, too. She's been depressed about her ankle and . . ." Her voice trailed off for a second. "And the fact that we kinda accused her of being the spy."

"That's fine," Charlie agreed.

"But no Triple," Allie J added quickly. "She might tell."

Charlie smiled. "Deal."

Allie texted Skye, and just a few minutes later, Skye limped through the bathroom door, blond waves bouncing around her shoulders.

"Um, knock knock," Skye rapped on the stall door. "What are you guys doing in the shower? Together."

"Come in!" Allie J pulled Skye into the steamy fold, then broke the news that C IS SPY via shaving cream.

Skye stomped her foot in a lavender-scented puddle. "I told you it wasn't me!" She looked more relieved than surprised. "So who are you going to turn in next? My ankle is getting much better, by the way. I can show you."

"Don't worry." Allie J turned up the pressure on the shower so that it ran at a loud *hiiisssssssssss* and leaned in. "That's the point. She's on our side. She's gonna to help us see the boys."

"Why would she do that?" Skye asked Allie J, as if Charlie weren't sitting right there.

"Because she's not as bad as we thought," Allie J explained.

Charlie's insides warmed, and it wasn't from the shower steam.

Skye sat down on the stall bench, downgrading her stare from murderous to curious. "Why are we talking about this in the shower?"

Allie J shot Charlie a nod-glance. Charlie lifted the gold skeleton key and winked.

"What's that?" Skye asked.

"Shhhhhhh," Allie J and Charlie hissed at the same time.

Charlie reached for the can. It was almost empty. She shook it twice and managed to eke out enough foam to write: *TUNNEL BOYS.*

Skye's white-blond brows slammed together in bewilderment. "Ohmuhgud, what are you talking about?"

"Trust us, it's good," Allie J explained, and then mouthed, "Taz." Skye's brows drifted back into place.

"Why are you doing this?" Just as Allie J had, Skye asked the inevitable. Charlie couldn't blame either of them.

"Because it's like we're living on some kind of reality show," Charlie said quietly. "I'm tired of being watched and forced to compete against people who could be my friends. This ridiculous competition isn't what anyone signed on for, and I want to do something about it. I want to go to a place where we can just hang out and be normal. Dial down the drama and—"

"Make out," Allie J blurted, then dialed back her enthusiasm. "Sorry," she said to Charlie.

"It's okay, I told you. We're done." *For now, anyway.*

Skye smiled radiantly. "When you put it that way . . . I'm in."

"You have to agree to some things first." Charlie smoothed her hands over the frizz formerly known as her hair. "First, no more Charlie Brown-nose."

The girls nodded in agreement.

"Second, we trust each other completely."

Allie J tried to write a check mark on the wall, but a little slanted foam line was all the can had left to give.

"And third, full disclosure about everything," Charlie added, knowing that she was still holding back one more secret: Why she'd really broken up with Darwin. Or rather, how she hoped that one day in the future, when he'd grown tired of Allie J, they would still end up together. But that was hers to keep.

"Deal?"

"Deal," the girls responded.

"So when are we you-know-what-ing with you-know-who?" Skye might have been as beautiful as a Bond girl, but the girl did not speak spy.

"Tonight," Charlie promised.

A smile started to stretch across Skye's face, but it stopped at a grimace. "Uh-oh."

"What?" Allie J asked. Her eyes were as round as the pesos in the wall, as if she were anticipating major disappointment.

"Toes before bros," Skye pouted. "I'm supposed to coach some dancers."

"So meet us after," Charlie suggested.

"Thanks." Skye smiled brightly.

"Sure." Charlie could feel her feet expanding from the heat, and if she wasn't mistaken, her heart had a little more volume too. So this was what having friends felt like? "Let's make a pact. What we're doing is dangerous, and we need to have each other's backs. We have to protect each other and our secret. To the grave!"

"The grave!" Allie J and Skye agreed.

Charlie didn't bother hiding her grin. On a campus where everything was an illusion, she had finally found something real.

24

Skye had been elevating her swollen ankle on the barre for the last twenty-eight minutes. It was the longest she had ever balanced flamingo style, and she imagined her muscles were aching pretty badly. But she couldn't feel a thing. As always, pain faded into the background like a shy friend when she was doing what she loved.

"Lead with your torso, Tweety!" Skye shouted over the jazz music. "Not your head."

Tweety nodded like she understood, then proved it.

"Perfect!" Skye called. "Did you feel the difference?"

"Totally!" Tweety chirped with glee. "Thanks!"

"What about me?" Ophelia asked, mid-pivot.

"Ever since we twisted your hair into Princess Leia buns your balance has been much better," Skye called. "You've got it!"

"Now me," Sadie pant-asked, her choppy Robot oiled to a smooth slice.

"Keep carving butter and Mimi will love it."

With each critique, Skye could feel her inner alpha returning. Even the color of her ankle was fading from purple to rotten banana yellow–ish brown.

"Prue, what are you chewing?" Skye winced.

Prue blush-swallowed. "A bran bar."

"Why?" Skye asked, and then remembered Mimi's suggestion. "I don't think she literally meant 'loosen up.' She probably wanted to see more hips and less spine. Can you try that?"

Prue swayed like Shakira, practically knocking out a window with her sharp ilium bone. It was clear the ballet prodigy was having a hard time adapting to the free flow of jazz.

"Okay." Skye took a patient inhale. "Imagine your hips are a pot filled with water," she tried. "What you want to do is shake the water from side to side without spilling it. Try again."

Prue tried and spilled.

"Again."

Spuh-lat! Prue spilled.

"Again."

Prue sloshed and wobbled and spilled . . .

. . . and then she got it.

Everyone burst into applause.

"Yes!" Skye shouted, good tears pinching the back of her

eyes. She wanted to dance for joy but settled for a series of enthusiastic single-leg knee bends. "Music louder!" she commanded. "Let's keep going."

Sadie launched into a tour jeté–pirouette followed by a donkey kick.

"Ride the beat, Sadie, don't just hit it!"

Sadie smiled her thanks.

All of a sudden, a series of vibrations shocked through Skye's leg. *Ohmuhgud!* Were her limbs seizing? Had she just fulfilled her destiny? Was it time to die? She forced herself to make eye contact with the site of the leg shake, fearing the worst about what she would find there.

Instead of a gangrenous thigh, Skye saw the aPod in her hip holster, flashing in emergency mode. She had five urgent messages. Every one of them was from Charlie. Most of them said **WHERE R U?????** The other two were something about a map.

Skye's forehead stung with *how could I possibly have spaced on this* sweat. It was almost 9:00 p.m. She'd been so wrapped up in the session, she'd completely lost track of the time. But wait—hadn't she just made a pledge with herself? Toes before bros? Now here she was cutting the lesson short to sneak off and see Taz. But it was more than Taz. This was about the new pact she'd made with Charlie and Allie J.

Or at least that was what she told herself.

"Music off!" Skye clapped sharply. "Okay, you're done. Mimi is going to be so impressed."

"Wait!" Ophelia cried. "My turnout isn't quite right yet."

"Yeah, and my leaps still have lead," Sadie whined.

Skye's ankle began throbbing. She felt more torn than cheap tights. "I really have to go."

"Where?" Prue stiffened. "Did your spy signal beep?"

"Huh?" Skye squinted like she was hard of hearing.

"We heard you were the spy." Ophelia loosened her side buns. "And it kinda makes sense. You're useless with that ankle, but you're still here. It sort of adds up. Why else would Shira keep you?" She shook out her thick black hair. "No offense."

"Um, is coaching you useless?" Skye managed, despite what felt like a balled-up leg warmer in the back of her throat. "'Cause from where I'm limping, you needed more saving than the beluga whales."

"Then why are you going?" Sadie zipped up her silver sweatshirt and flipped the metallic hood over her head.

"I just have to do something, okay?" The backs of Skye's eyes pinched again, but this time it was the bad tears. The girls who'd just been hanging on her every word were now hanging her out to dry. It hurt like doing the splits in skinny jeans.

"What?" Tweety asked, cocking her ample head. "Like spy?"

For a split second Skye considered dropping Charlie's name to clear her own. But they'd made a pact. There had to be another way. "I'm not the spy, okay?" She sniffled.

"Oh, cry me a Riverdance," Prue challenged. "Prove it!"

"Fine!" Skye snapped, reaching for her aPod. "I will."

Skye: B there in 5!

Her thumb went white as she rage-pressed the SEND button. "Let's go!"

Skye hobbled out of the studio with a pack of four dancers following her lead, possibly for the very last time.

25

ALPHA ACADEMY
THE DARK
WEDNESDAY, SEPTEMBER 8TH
8:28 P.M.

The night air smelled like a passing rainstorm even though it had been sunny all day.

"So how do you know so much about this place?" Allie scurried to keep up with Charlie as they darted across the dark campus. Charlie had somehow orchestrated a campus-wide blackout to keep the surveillance camera from seeing them. Even the moon was cooperating.

Charlie stopped and looked squarely into Allie's green eyes. "Truth?"

Allie nodded earnestly, like truth was something she practiced every day. *Ha!*

"I invented a lot of this island."

"Liar!" Allie blurted. "There's no way! I assumed Shira brought in some inventors from the future."

"Nope." Heavy sadness fluttered over Charlie's eyelids, forcing them downward. "More like someone from her past."

She swallowed. "But Shira can never know. She thinks it came from her research and development team. If she found out I used her lab . . ." Charlie finger-sliced her neck. "The people who need to know about my . . . abilities . . . do. And that's enough for me." She blinked like she was lying to herself. Of course she wanted Shira to know. Who wouldn't?

Allie studied Charlie's face for the first time. It was perfectly symmetrical. Her skin was clear. Her dark eyes were soothing. Her lips were full (enough). She was like that sketch of a woman's face Allie had once gotten at the MAC counter. The makeup artist had brushed colors over the sketch's eyelids, cheeks, and lips, demonstrating the proper way to apply the latest palates. Once she was done, the drawing's bland features came to life. In Charlie's case, it wasn't makeup that had brightened her face—it was skill. And it upgraded her beauty to the kind people wanted to stare at.

Just like Trina with her art.

"Honest-leh," Allie exclaimed. "This is amazing. You're so . . . smart. I can't believe Darwin broke up—" She stopped herself before her callused bare foot got stuck in her mouth. But it was too late.

Charlie smiled like someone about to cry, then picked up the pace.

"I didn't mean that. Well, I did, but I didn't mean to mention him." Allie scampered behind like an eager puppy.

"It's not like he's into me anyway," she panted, immediately regretting her insensitivity. Charlie, of all people, should not be expected to stroke Allie's ego. Not when it came to Darwin. But he was Allie's hot stove and she couldn't resist touching it. Even if it meant coming off as a self-absorbed lovesick desperado to her new friend who just so happened to be his ex.

Charlie unlocked the fence that protected the organic vegetable garden from salad-obsessed alphas. "Hurry, get in."

Allie slipped in, almost gagging on the moist, muddy smell of earth—a smell often associated with slimy worms. Worms who were probably gearing up to wiggle over her bare feet and lay eggs under her toenails . . .

"So why do you think Darwin doesn't like you anymore?" Charlie asked, closing the gate behind them. Allie considered asking where they were going but didn't dare change the subject.

"He didn't look at me in class the other day. Not once. And he never bothered to text after I bolted."

Charlie led them through two rows of onions. "What happened to you?"

Allie shrugged. "Keifer hated what I wrote, and I was embarrassed. I'm, um, used to creating alone in the wilderness. And this feels like speed-dating, only with writing, and it's not working for me. I'm blocked. So I ran off to reconnect with nature."

The truth was, the muse from Oprah had found Allie sobbing under an açaí palm, and she'd pretended she was lost. She'd been thinking about how happy Darwin and Charlie's toes had looked when they found each other in the sand. And now, standing in the shadow of Charlie's genius, Allie felt like running all over again. How could she possibly impress Darwin when he'd had Charlie first? It was like buying makeup at Bath & Body Works after a lifetime of Chanel.

"I don't even know why I'm on this secret mission. It's not like he wants to see me." Tears came all over again. At least this time she could blame it on the onions.

Charlie crouched down by a bed of lettuce. "What are you talking about?"

"I was supposed to meet him the other night—but he never showed." Allie sniffled.

"I wouldn't worry about how Darwin was acting." She snapped off a crisp leaf of romaine and used it to clear away a soil pile. "Shira's been tracking her sons with cameras. The feed goes straight to digital picture frames in her office. Darwin knew he was being watched and didn't want to get busted, that's all."

A cool breeze snaked by Allie's cheek and her heart lifted in her chest. "So he might still like me?"

"He definitely does." Charlie didn't look at her as she cleared away another scoop of mud. Traces of silver glittered between the brown muck, and suddenly a hatch appeared. Charlie yanked the handle.

"Whoa," Allie gasped, wishing she had a better vocabulary. But what else does one say when someone lifts up a hatch in an organic vegetable garden that leads to a seemingly endless, underground spiral staircase?

A new sense of purpose filled Allie. She wasn't just along for the ride, hoping for one last look at a boy with a fetching lip freckle. She was back in the driver's seat, speeding toward a make-out session with a boy who made Fletcher look like Tofurky—a less appetizing substitute for the real thing.

But it wasn't just Darwin-joy that made her want to jump down the spiral steps two at a time. It was Charlie-joy, too. They were becoming friends, and it had been a while since she'd had one of those.

"Follow me." Charlie slipped inside. "Leave the hatch slightly open for Skye."

Allie shimmied in after her. "Eeeeeeeeee," she squealed. "It's freezing in here." Her breath puffed from her lips like cigar smoke. She stepped onto the cold cement step, wondering what kind of bacteria lay in waiting. But an itchy foot was a small price to pay for love.

"Press alpha-H on your aPod," Charlie whispered. "Your uniform will heat up."

"Ahhhhhh." Allie sighed like she was finally peeing after driving from California to Oregon.

"Shira thinks the cold will keep her skin from aging."

"In bed." Allie giggled.

Charlie giggled back.

"So how do we let the boys know we're here?"

Charlie kept winding down the steps, her brown hair swishing back and forth across the back of her champagne-colored blouse. "Whenever Darwin and I snuck out to meet each other, I sent him a song from a fake e-mail address with an untraceable IP address."

Allie felt a flicker of jealousy despite Charlie's assurances. Charlie and Darwin had secret codes. She and Fletch hadn't even bothered to coordinate ringtones. The most romantic thing they'd ever done was get matching highlights.

"So what was your song?" Allie asked like someone who never got jealous.

"'We Belong Together' by Mariah Carey." Charlie shrugged matter-of-factly. "We kind of had goofy songs for everything. 'I Turn My Camera On' by Spoon when Shira's tattling assistant was lurking. 'SOS' by Rihanna for 'meet me after Shira's done torturing you.' Weezer's 'Say It Ain't So' when Dingo was about to pull a prank. But Mariah was the default."

Allie's mind expanded with questions like a cooked bag of Jiffy Pop. The stove was burning hotter than ever and she had to touch it. "So what if Darwin gets your message and thinks you're the one coming to meet him? Will he think you want to get back together? Will he be upset when he sees it's me and not you?"

"Don't worry," Charlie said with certainty as she sent the message. But instead of Mariah, she sent him "Meet Me at Midnight" by Allie J. The subject line said VEGGIE TUN-NEL. "Darwin's smart," she said. "He'll figure it out."

Charlie punched some numbers in the side of her skeleton key, then inserted the A-shaped end into a slot to the right of the door. The slot glowed bright neon blue, and the cement door immediately lifted open, revealing a large vestibule and a ski-lift chair waiting to whisk them toward the boys.

"This is serious-leh amazing," Allie gushed.

They were who-knew-how-many feet underground. Dozens of tunnels branched out in all directions like tracks at a busy train station, only they were hewn from glass, not concrete. Eerie blue light waved all around them, making pale Charlie look like she was a member of the Blue Man Group. Allie realized with a jolt that the glow came from the walls—which were actually those of a giant aquarium. In the ceiling overhead, the walls next to her, and the chilly glass beneath her feet swam thousands of the most exotic, colorful fish Allie could possibly have imagined.

Charlie checked her aPod. "Skye's really late. Do you think something happened?"

Allie couldn't bring herself to respond. The splendor

of her surroundings was too much to process. It was more romantic than Disneyland at night.

Just then a loud BAAAAMMMM echoed through the tunnels. Footsteps and whispers followed. Schools of fish scattered. Allie's heart revved.

BAAAAMMM!

Charlie retrieved her skeleton key from her pocket. The door lowered and the lights shut off. They were trapped inside. "Hide!"

"Where?" Allie panicked.

"Shhhhhh," Charlie hissed.

Allie pressed her back up against the nearest wall-slash-aquarium. Was the glass double-paned? Were the fish trying to break through? Was the water seeping out of the aquarium into the tunnels, where it would surely flood and drown her? The air was thick and sticky, and each breath felt like she was snorting a milk shake. She was no longer part of a beautiful seascape. She was encased in glass, trapped in Sleeping Beauty's coffin.

Just like in the fairy tale, a kiss was inevitable. But would it be her true love's—or the kiss of death?

Bam! Bam!

The footsteps were getting closer. She'd have her answer soon.

26

Charlie locked hands with Allie J in the dark. They were pressed up against the aquarium on the tunnel just left of the vestibule, and Allie J kept muttering something about milk shakes.

BAAAAAM!

They squeezed harder.

BAAAAAM!

And harder.

If Shira caught Allie J, she'd go back to her fans and successful career. Big deal. But Charlie? She'd be on the next PAP to some boarding school in New Jersey with no hope of ever seeing Darwin again.

"What should we do?" Allie J chattered.

"Shhhhh," Charlie hissed, more frustrated with herself than with the songstress. She usually had all the answers. And now, when she needed them most, she—

"Charlie?" a familiar voice whisper-called through the concrete door.

"Skye?" Charlie and Allie J giggle-sighed with relief.

"Let me in!"

Charlie reinserted the key into the padlock. It flashed once. The lights flickered on, and the door began to lift slowly.

A flurry of footsteps sounded in the outer vestibule. Either an octopus was on the loose, or Skye was not alone.

"Great directions," she limped forward.

"Hello, pretty, pretty fishy." A red-haired bun-head tapped on the glass, drawing a heart with her polished fingers around a yellow-and-blue swimmer.

"Wow. This place is amazing," said the pretty Hawaiian girl. Charlie recognized her and the one with the big head from the spa. "It feels like we're in a video game."

"See, I told you I wasn't the spy. Would a spy bring you here?" Skye flashed a knowing wink at Charlie, like their secret was still safe with her.

HA!

"You brought them here to prove you're not a spy?" Charlie snapped.

"Yup." Skye nodded proudly and knelt to examine a little puffer fish beneath the floor. "And they believe me now, right?"

The bun-heads nodded yes, still marveling at their surroundings.

"So where are the boys?" asked a girl with pencil-straight posture.

Charlie lowered the temperature on her uniform to keep from boiling over. She had never been so angry in her life: not when Taz head-bombed her Popsicle-stick replica of the Empire State Building; not when that little boy in Greece swiped her backpack; and not when Shira ripped the picture of Darwin out of her cameo bracelet. Because those people hadn't taken her trust and tap-danced all over it. They'd never pledged friendship. They'd promised her nothing. And Skye had.

"What are you doing?" Charlie demanded. "This was supposed to be a secret thing. We said to the grave, remember?"

"I know, I'm sorry. But they won't tell." Skye smiled innocently. "They promised."

"Just like you did?" Charlie snapped.

"You're so cute!" Ophelia, oblivious to the argument, pressed her lips against the glass and kissed a pearly pink starfish.

"See? They're totally harmless." Skye looked at Charlie with big pleading turquoise eyes.

Charlie opened her mouth to scream, but couldn't. What was it about pretty girls that made them so impossible to reprimand? It felt like smacking a flower.

"If we get caught, it's your fault," Charlie hissed.

"Don't worry." Skye limped forward and tried to hug her. "I never get caught."

Charlie didn't hug back. One lone eel slithered under their feet. Maybe Shira was right. Maybe there was no such thing as true friends—just relatives and contacts. And if that was true, she had nothing to gain by sharing the tunnels.

"Mission off!" Charlie barked.

"What?" the redhead squeaked.

Skye's eyes widened with hurt, like Charlie actually had smacked her.

"It's too risky." She nudged everyone back through the door to the staircase, then activated the skeleton key.

The bun-heads began moaning their disappointment.

"I told you, Charlie," Skye urged. "I never get—"

But it was too late. The door began to close. Just before it shut they heard the *whooosh* of the chairlift as it sped off.

"Whoooooo!" Allie J called. "See yaaaaaa!"

"Allie J, no!" Charlie cried. But the dark-haired singer was gone. How had she not noticed Allie J had left the group?

"We need to go after her," Skye said, her eyes wide with hope. "What if she gets into trouble and needs us?"

The girls nodded their agreement.

Charlie knew their pleas had more to do with chasing down the boys. But at the same time, Skye had a point. Allie J shouldn't be down there alone.

With a reluctant sigh, Charlie reinserted the key.

"RE-JECT-ED!"

"What?" she gasped. Her insides melted to wobbly goo.

She entered the code again: 2-4-2-7-5-4-3

"RE-JECT-ED!"

2-4-2-7-5-4-3

"RE-JECT-ED!" 2-4-2-7-5-4-3

"RE-JECT-ED!"

Charlie covered her mouth, warding off the panic-puke. "Oh. My. God. Shira knows."

As if on cue, all five of their aPods beeped.

SHIRA: ASSEMBLY IN 20 MINUTES. REPORT TO THE PAVILION.

"Ohmuhgod!"

"What are we going to do?"

"Run!"

Everyone raced for the hatch.

Skye grabbed Charlie's arm frantically. "What about Allie J?"

"We can't help her now," Charlie replied coldly. After all, Darwin was great in a crisis. He would take good care of her.

But as usual, Charlie was on her own.

27

Skye wasn't the only one who found God in the Pavilion.
Alpha lips were moving at a frenzied pace as the remaining
girls—minus Allie J, who was still missing—prayed for sal-
vation amid the random claps of thunder.

"It's gonna be me." Charlie bit her thumbnail. All the
lights on campus were back on, blindingly bright, like an
interrogation room. "I'm the one who stole the key and
brought everyone down there."

"Yeah, but it's my second offense." Skye rolled her swollen ankle. The pain had lowered to a three. "Besides, I can't
even dance. So what good am I?"

"You have a point there," Triple scoffed, examining her
hair extensions for split ends. Her lack of anxiety made
Skye hate her even more. Or was that jealousy? If Skye had
half of Triple's discipline, this contest would be over by now.
But she didn't. Not even close. And now her mother and

everyone in Westchester would know she didn't have drive to back her talent. Sure, Madame P would probably still use her as an example in dance class—an example of failure.

The thunder was getting louder. Shira was on her way.

"Maybe it'll be Allie J," Skye whispered to Charlie. "She's not even here."

Charlie didn't bother to turn her head. "Maybe."

Even though Skye had apologized fifty times, Charlie was still mad about the surprise guests. All Skye could do now was talk to Charlie like everything was okay between them. And eventually it would be. It was a technique she'd used dozens of times on her friends back home and it always worked. "You think Shira will notice Allie J's not here?"

"I took care of it, okay?" Charlie whisper-hissed. She nodded to a chair in the back. A girl with jet-black hair and green eyes was reading her aPod.

"Allie J!" Skye cried.

"Shhhh!" Charlie warned. "It's just a hologram."

"How cool." Skye tried to smile, but she had a feeling it came off as more of a frown. If Allie J was "there," Skye was back at the top of the hit list.

A band girl dragging a midsize wheelie hurried by.

Skye filled with hope.

"What's with the suitcase?" she asked. "Convinced you're going home?"

"No, this is my clarinet." The girl gave a nervous laugh.

"There's been tons of sabotage in the wind section. I can't leave home without it."

"I know what you mean." Charlie nodded knowingly. "You can't trust anyone around here." She shot a pointed look at Skye.

Skye's ankle throbbed and she fought the urge to roll her eyes. It wasn't a matter of trust. She hadn't set out to break their pact. She just wanted it all—dancers, boys, friendship, and adventure. Wasn't that the alpha way?

"Charlie, I . . ." She wanted to apologize again, but the words tasted more fake and cheesy than Kraft Singles. She wasn't sorry for bringing the dancers. They trusted her now. She was just sorry that her actions had made Charlie so mad. And that wasn't an easy thing to explain.

"Students." Shira's voice boomed throughout the room, silencing everyone immediately.

Skye dutifully began clapping along with the others.

"I expected more." Red hair flew wildly around her shoulders. She looked like a demon about to feed.

Skye's limbs tingled in fear. The sting of adrenaline warned her that danger lay ahead. Her body couldn't run . . . but her mind did. There were so many things she hadn't done yet.

I never learned to fly a PAP.

I never made it to the zoo to pet the baby animals.

I never lip-kissed Taz.

I never got to show Mimi what I'm made of.

I never got to star in a dance performance.

I never made my mom proud.

The last thought made Skye ache all over.

Onstage, Shira was stomping around. "I started this academy because I grew tired of seeing potential alphas on TMZ, dancing on tables and falling out of cars without underwear. Who they were wearing or dating or drinking became more important than what they were actually doing with their lives." Shira's hair settled on her shoulders like a bird landing on a perch. "I hold you to a higher standard. My standard. And I demand that you back up your extraordinary talent with extraordinary judgment."

Skye massaged her restless legs. *Just tell us already!*

"There is a time for mating. After all, the world always needs more alphas. But that time is not now." Shira gazed out over the crowd.

A bolt of lightning sliced through the air, just missing the PAP landing outside.

"When you break a rule, you break my trust. If I can't trust you, you don't belong here."

Triple nodded in agreement. Charlie twirled her bracelets. Skye was too scared to move.

A sharp pain sliced through her ankle. Like her grandmother's arthritic wrist could predict rain, Skye's soreness told her something major was on the way.

She leaned forward in her chair. So did Triple, Charlie, hologram Allie J, and everyone else in the room.

Shira opened her mouth to speak.

EEEEEEEEEEP!

Huh?

Shira lifted her aPod from the pocket of her billowing black dress. Fiona raced onstage and whispered in her ear. Shira's face darkened, her brows furrowing behind her lenses. Thunder rolled and lightning crashed.

"Ahhhh!" the clarinet girl screamed, breaking under the pressure.

Shira looked up at the audience, as if remembering they were there. "We will reconvene in the morning at 7 a.m. sharp."

Skye and the others gasped as Shira cliffhangered their night. Every cell in Skye's body was firing. She wasn't sure she could last another minute without knowing her fate.

"Enjoy this night, ladies," Shira said as she walked off the stage. "It might be your last."

Half an hour later, Skye lay in bed, balling her fluffy, star-speckled comforter in her sweaty fists. Triple Threat was purring peacefully, knowing she was safe. Charlie flipped from side to side trying to get comfortable. And hologram Allie J was fast asleep.

Skye begged her inner self for an explanation. Something to help her understand why she had such a hard time following rules. Why she couldn't be disciplined, like her mom, or dedicated, like Triple. She balled up her sleeves and whipped them across the room. Why bother with self-expression when the "self" she was expressing always got her in trouble?

Staring at the empty lavender slipper hanging from her lamp, Skye couldn't help but think that her hopes and dreams were a waste of time. Unless . . .

Unless tonight's interrupted assembly was a second chance. An opportunity for her to prove to herself and the world that she could power down her fun button and crank up the serious.

And if she was getting a second chance, she was going to do it right.

New HAD No. 1: To stay at Alpha Academy.

New HAD No. 2: To earn Charlie's forgiveness.

New HAD No. 3: To heal and dance by morning.

New HAD No. 4: To swear off boys until graduation.

New HAD No. 5: To be my the best.

Skye folded up each piece of paper and slipped them into the shoe's not-so-secret compartment, then lassoed it around the lamp. It swung back and forth, back and forth, back and forth . . . a bitter reminder that her hopes and dreams were hanging by a thin, fraying ribbon.

28

Later that night, Allie stepped out of the hatch. She was back in the worm-infested mud. Only this time she didn't think of disease. She thought of love.

The night air was electrified—and so was Allie. She was tingling from her freshly kissed lips down to her unkempt toes. She wanted to squeal with glee, but aPod beat her to it. It pinged to life with seventeen new messages. Seventeen?

SHIRA: ASSEMBLY IN TWENTY MINUTES. REPORT TO THE PAVILION.

Charlie: Where r u?

Skye: R u okay?

Charlie: I left the hatch open. Leave the way we came.

Skye: What does the tunnel look like?

Charlie: Y aren't u txting back?

Skye: Is Taz there?

Charlie: Darwin should know the exits.

Skye: Hurry up! Shira is going to cut someone!

Skye: Charlie made a hologram of u so Shira won't know u r gone

Skye: Kiss Darwin bc you could be cut

Skye: Seriously, where r u?

Charlie: Allie J?! Where r u?

Skye: No one cut yet. Shira had emergen-c. Found the person who stole her sense of humor. ☺

Charlie: Just put your hologram to bed. It's sleeping beside Triple.

Skye: Your hologram is snoring.

Charlie: Coast is clear. Come back now if u can.

Fear coursed through her body as she read the urgent texts, her heart rate elevating with each one. She was about to panic. And then one more came through.

Darwin: U OK?

Allie J: Never better. ☺

She smiled to herself, reviewing the night's events frame by frame like a DVD:

The chairlift whisking her through the aquarium tunnels.

Knowing she should scream but giggling instead. What she's doing is crazy, risky, dangerous, and exciting.

As if sensing the presence of another person, the chair slows. And then stops. Darwin gently places his guitar on the glass floor, then offers his hand and helps her down.

The chair lingers like a nosy parent.

Darwin pops a cinnamon-scented toothpick between his lips.

Allie's breath seizes in her chest.

Darwin asks her to sit. He admits it takes him months to write songs. Says he understands why she keeps buckling in class. Wishes there wasn't so much pressure to perform, says pressure is passion's poison.

Darwin plays the first song he ever wrote in one day, says it was inspired by her. It's called "Pressure Is Passion's Poison."

The lyrics have something to do with a beautiful girl . . . green eyes . . . filled with passion . . .

The rest of the lyrics fall away. He had her at "beautiful."

He strums his last strum. Fletcher's face finds its way into Allie's head. Allie closes her eyes to make it go away. A whiff of cinnamon. A shadow over her face. Warm lips. They're not Fletcher's. They're better than Fletcher's! They're . . . who's Fletcher?

Allie is floating . . .

She floats when Darwin puts her back in the chair . . .

Floats when he kisses her again . . .

Floats when he triple-taps the chair and tells it to take good care of his special girl . . .

Then she floats up the winding staircase . . .

And considers asking him to call her plain old Allie instead of— "Allie J?"

A stern voice sounded behind her, and Allie crashed back down to the very muddy earth. Her throat tightened like she was wearing a toddler's turtleneck, and she turned around slowly . . . and came face-to-face with the muse from Oprah; the same one who'd found her crying under the açaí after class.

"Lost again?" The muse tapped her foot impatiently.

"Uh-h," Allie stammered, taking a step backward. *Think, think, think.* "I, uh, I'm expecting a package from my mom.

It's medicine. For my condition. I was looking for the mail-room, but it can wait until morning, so I'll just go back to my house and use what I have left and—"

"Nonsense." The muse's scowl relaxed into a smile. "When it comes to health, leave nothing to chance."

"Okay then." Allie began walking away. "Thanks. I'll go get it then. G'night."

"You can't possibly walk all the way to Shira's office from here."

"Shira's office?" Allie's cinnamon-flavored lips dried.

"Yes," the muse said as if it should have been obvious. "All packages go through her." She powered up her hover-disc. "Hop on, I'll take you."

Before Allie could refuse, she was floating again. Only this time it did not feel good.

29

Allie shifted restlessly in the waiting-room chair, trying to get comfortable. Outside, campus was all lit up, and lightning illuminated the sky. Inside, her heart was racing. How could she possibly explain her quest for medicine at this hour? Shira had all of her records. She knew Allie J was in perfect health.

The Oprah muse paced outside Shira's door, wringing her hands and shooting deadly glares at Allie whenever she could. Unlike Thalia, she offered no hope. In fact, her mannerisms suggested the exact opposite.

All Allie could do to keep from fainting was think of Darwin's kiss and hope that his mother found her half as charming as he did.

But wait? What was the big deal? She'd just casually stroll into the office and tell Shira she was on a writing bender. And that sometimes when bending, she'd wander around alone in the night consumed by the spirit within her. She could say it was something that happened during her creative voyages and that she didn't remember anything about medicine. How hard could it be? After all, she was a pretty decent liar. The fact that she was still there, masquerading as some green-blooded songstress was proof of that. Who knew? Maybe she'd end up bonding with Shira. Maybe they'd become—

Shira's office door clicked open.

Allie stood to greet her new mentor. But it wasn't Shira who walked out. It was a girl.

The girl wasn't beautiful, but she wasn't ugly, either. Her jet-black hair was shiny and parted down the middle. Her skin was pale. Her eyes were green. Her dress was white. Her feet were bare. Her left cheek was dotted with a single mole . . .

Suddenly, Allie's limbs turned weightless. Her forehead began to bead with sweat. Her tongue swelled.

"Whoa." The girl scanned her top to bottom. "The odds are slim, but you could be my twin."

Allie remained still. The room started spinning. Her ears rang.

"Allie A. Abbott"—the Oprah muse turned to Allie with a catty grin—"meet Allie J. Abbott. Shira will see you now."

Allie turned to run. But before she could lift her feet off the glass floor, the world went black.

30

SHIRA'S OFFICE
WEDNESDAY, SEPTEMBER 8TH
11:59 P.M.

The arresting smell of spicy coffee beans and—*was that cayenne pepper and maple syrup?*—sucked Allie from the swirling darkness. Her eyelids were heavier than an overnight bag. Her tongue felt like a dry dirt path, her teeth tiny rocks that had been kicked aside by mindless hikers.

"Where am I?" she croaked.

"*Who* are you, is a better question," the woman stood, taking the coffee smell with her.

"Huh?"

"Don't bother answering now." She paced. "You'll have plenty of time for that later, Allie Ayyyyyyyyyyyyyyyyy." She drew out the A sound.

"Huh?" Trepidation washed through Allie's insides like a colonic. *What was happening? Why was she here?*

"While identity theft is illegal it does prove you have do-or-die determination: a crucial Alpha quality."

She picked up a framed photo of Darwin. The sight of him filled Allie with a liquid Theraflu-type warmth. Her lips tingled and her heart swayed like a puppy wagging its tail.

"My Shira-instincts are telling me to keep you at the Academy. But the true test of your . . ." Shira paused to push the dark glasses up her nose, ". . . alphaness will come with what you do next."

"Whaddaya mean?" Allie asked, unable to look away from the picture.

"I *mean* only a true alpha could survive telling her teachers, friends, and . . ." she placed the photo of her son back on the shelf, ". . . anyone else who may have believed you were a talented singer-songwriter-environmentalist. . . " Shira grinned, a fox finishing off its last bite of lamb. "So now it is time for Allie Ayyyyy to do what Allie Jayyyyy has done her entire life."

"What's that?" Allie croaked.

"Face the music." Shira winked.

An invisible knife stabbed Allie's wagging heart. *How could she step foot back in Jackie O? What would her roommates say? Would Darwin ever forgive her? Would he still like her? What if Trina and Fletcher found out?*

Everything was coming back to her now.

Everything but hope.

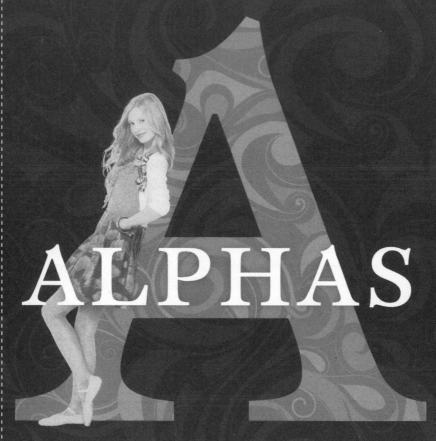

Once upon a time, there were four betas just waiting for their alpha.

It took a miracle to bring the Pretty Committee together—or rather, a New Year's Yves party. Because sometimes when you meet someone, it just *cliques*.

CHARMED AND DANGEROUS
The CLIQUE Prequel

Special Hardcover Edition Coming 10•27•09

Welcome to Poppy.

A poppy is a beautiful blooming red flower
(like the one on the spine of this book). It is also
the name of the home of your favorite books.

Poppy takes the real world and makes it
a little funnier, a little more fabulous.

Poppy novels are wild, witty, and inspiring.
They were written just for you.

So sit back, get comfy, and pick a Poppy.

poppy

www.pickapoppy.com

THE A-LIST
HOLLYWOOD ROYALTY

gossip girl

THE CLIQUE

ALPHAS

SECRETS OF MY
HOLLYWOOD LIFE

the it girl

POSEUR